Can he

St. John Fotheringay-Phipps has nearly forgotten who he truly is. As the dashing, amusing dandy known to all in society as Fungy, he has hidden himself behind a mask of merriment. But he is reminded that there are pleasures beyond society -- when he finds himself feeling responsible for the innocently lovely and fiercely intellectual Rose, the daughter of a famed archaeologist, and her charming, if socially inept, family.

Rose Grace knows that she cannot gamble with her future. She has suddenly been thrust into the role of mother to her two young sisters, companion to her brilliant, distracted father --and family savior. She needs to do the right thing -- to forget her own desires and quickly find a wealthy husband before the creditors come beating at their door. Then why is she distracted by the foppishly handsome Fungy, who seems so very irresponsible and pleasure-loving? Surely he's the last person whose advice she should follow!

Can Rose wager her heart to help St. John find his way to the man he wants to be?

What Others have said about Dame Fortune

"Four Stars!" —*Romantic Times Book Club*

"Ms. Bond has proven to be a talented writer with a dab hand at creating interesting situations and lively dialogue." —*Jane Bowers, Romance Reviews Today*

"My eyes were glued to the pages as I read this wonderful story... a wonderful plot with amazing characters." —*Tangela Williams, Romance Reader's Connection*

"Loved It Enough to Buy It Twice" —*Priscilla Waaller, reader*

Books by Meredith Bond

The Merry Men Quartet: *The stories of four friends which just had to be told* (These books, originally published by Zebra Books, can be read in any order you choose, they are stand alone novels with recurring characters.)

An Exotic Heir (originally published as *Love of My Life*)

A Merry Marquis (originally published as *Miss Seton's Sonata*. Look for it in 2014)

A Rake's Reward (originally published as *Wooing Miss Whatley*. Look for it in 2014)

A Dandy in Disguise (originally published as *Dame Fortune*)

The Vallen Series:

Storm on the Horizon, a historical paranormal novella

Magic in the Storm, a Regency-set paranormal romance

"In A Beginning", a short story featuring Lilith

A Dandy in Disguise

Meredith Bond

Previously published as Dame Fortune
by Zebra Books

Copyright, September, 2013, Meredith Bond.
All rights reserved.

No part of this book may be reproduced or transmitted in any form by any means—graphic, electronic or mechanical—without permission in writing from the author, except by a reviewer who may quote brief passages in a review.

Published by Anessa Books, www.anessabooks.com.

ISBN-13: 978-1493572663

ISBN-10: 1493572660

Dedication

To my father, my greatest cheerleader.

Acknowledgements

A huge thank you to all of the people who read this book and gave me their comments and ideas on how to make it better: Barbara McGuire, Debra Dunbar and Dana Gunn. And a huge thank you to my editor who did an amazing job, Nina Banerji.

In order to please others, we lose our hold on our life's purpose.

– Epictetus

One word frees us of all the weight and pain in life. That word is love.

– Sophocles

Prologue

April, 1802

Sated after a delicious morning of lovemaking, St. John lifted himself up to rest on one elbow and looked into Georgiana's heavy–lidded eyes. Life could not get any better than this.

"*Nunc scio quid sit amor,* " he said, smiling at her, knowing how much it bothered her when he quoted the classics.

She scowled at him and waited for the translation.

"Now I know what love is," he explained, running his hand down her naked body. He loved that every curve of her soft velvety skin was as familiar to him as his own body.

"St. John..." Georgiana began.

"Georgiana..." St. John began at exactly the same time.

They both stopped and laughed. But Georgiana stopped laughing a bit too quickly.

Looking away from him, she got up and pulled on her shift. He hated this part of their time together, when she dressed herself. He so enjoyed seeing her, feeling her, being with her.

Inevitably, though, she reached for her corset "St. John, you may congratulate me. I have accepted a proposal of marriage," she said abruptly

St. John's breathing stopped. His heart stopped. He looked up at her to read her face, to see if perhaps she was teasing him, but her back was still toward him. Finally, he took a deep breath to try to dispel the tightness that had formed in his chest. Perhaps it was better that she was still turned away. She wouldn't see the pain he was certain was painting his face. He took another breath and tried to erase the shock from his eyes.

Heedless of his nudity, he got out of bed, gently turning Georgiana to face him. "I don't understand. I thought you loved me."

She gave him a sad smile and ran her hands up his chest. "You are so beautifully formed, just like one of those pictures you showed me in your book."

He caught her hands with one of his own and brought her chin up with the other, so that she was forced to look him in the eye.

"I love you," he said, letting the words come up from deep within his soul—to reverberate, hopefully, within hers.

Her eyes filled with tears. "I didn't want you to— didn't ask you to."

"But I do." He paused, trying to keep the pain from his voice. "And I thought you loved me."

"Marriage is not always about love, St. John. Sometimes it's about money or social position."

"I have money. Not a lot, but enough."

"Yes. But you do not have a position in society, and you never will."

She pulled away from him, and said quietly, "And you are only nineteen."

Not quietly enough. "And how old is he?" he asked, failing to keep the bitterness from his voice.

"Please, don't be that way."

"It's an honest question. "

She turned away, shrugging, "Older." Giving one last longing look at his body over her shoulder, she turned to finish dressing. "You should get dressed," she said quietly.

St. John just stood there for a minute, letting the pain cut through his heart.

"If I had a place in society, would you love me?" he asked, impetuously.

"I *do* love you, St. John, but I need to marry." She handed him his breeches and shirt from the floor.

"What do I need to do?"

"You need to get dressed," she said, smiling at him as he stood holding his clothes, but making no move to put them on.

"That's not what I meant."

"I know," she laughed. She had a beautiful laugh and he enjoyed making it bubble from her throat. But now was not a time for laughter.

Now he needed answers. Now he needed to know what he had to do to make her love him as much as he loved her.

He slipped on his breeches. "Georgiana, please, what can I do?"

He pulled his shirt over his head and hastily tucked it in while reaching for his neckcloth.

"There is nothing you can do, St. John. Lord Mirthwood has proposed and I have accepted. That's all there is to it."

"But surely... what if I gained a position in society? I can, you know, easily. My cousin is the Marquis of Merrick. He can help..."

She smiled and turned to help him tie his neckcloth. She always did a much better job of it than he ever did. "Well, if you want to join the beau monde, you should start by caring a bit more about your clothes and how you wear them."

"My clothes are quite fashionable! Why, I bought this waistcoat only last season—and I was assured that it was all the crack."

"Yes," she said slowly, concentrating on what she was doing. "But that was last season. Now the styles are different. You've got to keep up with the times, St. John." She reached for his 'fashionable' waistcoat and helped him into it. "And really, my dear, all this Latin and Greek... well, whoever heard of anyone in society quoting the classics? It just is not done, St. John. If you must read it, for God's sake, don't let anyone know!"

He struggled into his coat, once again with her help. Smoothing out the wrinkles, she told him, "You are an amazingly handsome man. If you dressed well and made some effort to be fashionable..."

"You want me to be a dandy?" he sneered, but the hurt in his voice was close to the surface.

"No, but you asked how you could gain a position in society, and I'm telling you."

She reached up and, with tender fingers, brushed back his dark blond hair as it fell over his forehead and into his eyes. Gently kissing his cheek, she said, "Good-bye, St. John. Lord Mirthwood and I shall be leaving for America within a few weeks. You won't see me again. Keep well and be happy."

St. John just stood looking at her, memorizing every nuance of her face, every movement of her body, even her scent, an unusual musky tone of rose. He caressed her velvety cheek and the thick hair that fell in long chestnut waves around her shoulders. He feathered his lips across hers ever so gently. "Adieu, then, my lady fair. Keep my heart well, for it goes with you."

Georgiana's quick answering smile, tinged with regret, lingered with him as he turned and made his way out the door of her bedroom.

He worked to keep his shoulders straight as he ran down the stairs. But by the time he reached the still-dark early morning street, his back straightened of its own accord as clear, cleansing resolution flooded him.

He would make himself worthy of her love. He would become just what she wanted him to be.

She was marrying an older man, she'd said. In no more than five years— an old man wouldn't last long in such a barbaric place as America—she would be back. In no more than five years, he would be all that she wanted and more. Then she would marry him.

One

Fifteen years later...

There had to be more than this, Rose Grace thought to herself. There had to be some way for there to be more.

For forty minutes now she'd sat on the side of the ballroom, watching other people laugh and chat with friends, while her chaperone, her elderly Aunt Farmington, had slowly nodded off to sleep next to her.

Her aunt was supposed to be introducing her to people, but most of those in the *ton* she knew were now either dead or had moved to their country homes to live out the end of their lives in the company of their grandchildren.

Rose chastised herself. That wasn't entirely true. Her grandmother's sister did have some friends who were still among the beau monde. It was just that they were her aunt's contemporaries, and so far none of them had shown any desire to introduce their younger relatives to Rose.

Sighing, twisting her bracelet around her wrist, and watching her own knee bounce up and down wasn't going to get her anywhere. This was a waste of time. She was *not* going to continue sitting here.

She stood and joined her father, who was chatting with a small group of gentlemen. She scrunched up her nose—one of them was wearing too much cologne.

A Dandy In Disguise

"Lord Pemberton–Howe, is this your daughter?" the man standing across the circle from her father asked, giving her a wet, loose lipped smile.

Rose's father turned from the man to glance at her. "Er, your grace."

Rose curtseyed, even though they hadn't been properly introduced as yet. Her father's social manners never were what one would hope, but then on an archaeological dig it didn't really matter as much.

"Is there something wrong with your company this evening, Miss Grace? Or are you simply a very devoted child?" the gentleman next to the duke asked, smiling at her in a very paternal manner.

"Oh, there is nothing wrong with the company, sir. I'm afraid I just don't know anyone," Rose admitted, a little embarrassed at the fact.

"Where is your aunt?" her father asked, frowning over her shoulder. "I thought she was supposed to be introducing you around."

"I don't believe she's used to staying out this late." Rose turned around to glance at the woman in question whose head was now lolling awkwardly to the side.

"Oh dear." Clearly her father had caught sight of her.

"Yes." Rose turned back to the gentlemen and said with an apologetic smile and a shrug, "*mia kaké arché kánei éna kakó télos* "

"I beg your pardon!" the duke sputtered. "Perhaps the reason why your aunt hasn't introduced you is because you have never been taught how to behave in public."

Rose's mouth dropped open.

"I beg your pardon, sir," her father started, his eyes narrowing with anger. Rose put a hand on his arm. "She is nattering on in some strange, unknown language," the man said, scowling down at her. "Either that, or she's lost her mind and speaking gibberish!"

"Strange? Unknown...?" Lord Pemberton–Howe began. Even Rose had to admit confusion.

"Are you questioning me?" The elder gentleman turned on her father. The color in his face began to rise as well, as did the volume of his voice. "Perhaps you are unaware, sir, of the position I hold in society?" The gentleman accentuated his words by looking down his nose at her papa.

Rose cringed. Her father was not used to being spoken down to.

"And perhaps you, sir, should have had a better education!" Lord Pemberton–Howe's voice carried strongly as well.

A short burst of laughter interrupted what was quickly becoming an ugly scene. Quite a few other people who had been standing nearby had turned toward them, eager to hear what the commotion was about.

"My Lord Duke, I believe the young lady was speaking Greek," the laughing gentleman said. He was considerably younger than the duke, and quite a sight. His coat was dark blue and fit him so closely it looked as if it had been painted onto his broad shoulders. His waistcoat, which was elegantly cut, was a deep red shot through with silver thread and simply quite dazzling. He dripped with watch fobs, and a quizzing glass hung from a bright red ribbon around his neck. Rose had never seen anyone dressed so boldly before—it was as if he had taken all of the fashion dictates to quite another level. If she squinted past the brightness, he was probably an extremely handsome gentleman, but it was

A Dandy In Disguise

a little difficult to see his face properly behind the ridiculously high points of his shirt.

But, even more remarkable than his clothes, was his demeanor. He practically exuded ennui, speaking slowly, as if he hadn't a care in the world. And yet, Rose felt that behind the bored façade, nothing seemed to pass by him unnoticed.

"Yes. Yes, that's correct." her father said. "A rather common quote, I would have assumed."

The older man's color started to fade back to normal. "Greek you say, Fungy? Can't say I've ever actually heard anyone speak the language. Read it just fine," he added pointedly at Rose's father.

"Mind, sir?" the younger gentleman asked Lord Pemberton–Howe.

"What?" Rose's father asked.

"Introduce us?"

"Oh! Yes, of course. Er, the Duke of Argyll, Lord Halsbury, Mr. Fotheringay–Phipps; my daughter, Miss Rose Grace."

The duke nodded curtly to Rose, and Lord Halsbury, a slightly rotund older gentleman gave her a fatherly little smile. But Mr. Fotheringay–Phipps, the extraordinarily well–dressed gentleman who had come to her rescue, took her hand and raised it to his lips, sending Rose's heart fluttering as the heat from his kiss scorched her fingers right through her glove.

And yet, while he was bowing, his bright blue eyes looked into hers with such good humor that Rose could not resist smiling back at him. She even felt an answering bubble of laughter springing up from inside of her. It was clear he had understood what she'd said.

This all seemed so odd to Rose. But somehow, she felt that this outrageously fashionable gentleman could understand. Somehow, he was the only one who seemed to understand that this was all a game—one he clearly enjoyed being a part of. It felt good to have such an unexpected ally.

"I am certain Miss Grace knows she should not speak in a foreign tongue in the presence of those who might not understand her," Mr. Fotheringay–Phipps said, still keeping his mischief-filled eyes on Rose. "Clearly, she did not realize that not everyone would recall the quote. Euripides, is it not? 'A bad beginning makes for a bad ending.' But surely it is too soon to make such a dire prediction. You must give yourself at least a little more time, Miss Grace."

"Is that what she said," the duke muttered to himself.

"You are very kind, Mr. Fotheringay–Phipps," Rose said, feeling her cheeks burn. How ridiculous she was being!

"Fungy, please," he returned, "all my friends call me Fungy. And I do hope that you will soon call me friend."

Oh, now she was really blushing. She ducked her head in a nod. How could one man be so charming! Surely, he was one of those her mother had warned her to stay away from.

Another gentleman standing at the edge of their group gave a little cough. "Er, couldn't help but overhearing, but —the younger Miss Grace might benefit from a lesson in proper social behavior as well."

Two

"Not that Miss Grace was speaking in another language. More, er, flirting actually," the gentleman continued, his speech more and more hesitant as Lord Pemberton–Howe's face took on an increasingly ruddy hue, "but... well... might have a word with her?"

His voice petered out as he noticed Lord Pemberton–Howe's hands tighten into fists. Rose knew that her father would not create a scene in public, but this piece of information, so soon after her own faux–pas, was clearly proving to be too much for him. She put a restraining hand on his arm.

"And who might you be, sir, to have met my daughter?" Lord Pemberton–Howe asked.

"Er, Pip Haston, at your service, sir." The gentleman bowed. "Was walking past a bookstore when she popped out. Nearly bowled straight into me, and then started giggling and talking at me, you know how girls do, only we hadn't been introduced. Said as much, so she stuck out her hand and *introduced herself*!"

Rose's father paled.

"Oh, dear. I'll speak with her, Papa. Tomorrow," Rose said, clutching more tightly on to her father's arm.

"How many daughters do you have, my lord?" Mr. Fotheringay–Phipps asked, turning the conversation quickly onto safer waters. Mr. Haston took advantage of the distraction to disappear into the crowd once more. Rose flashed Mr. Fotheringay–Phipps a quick smile of gratitude.

"Hmm? Oh, er, three. Rose is the eldest. And then there is Aglaia, and then Thalia."

Mr. Fotheringay–Phipps gave a delighted laugh. "Ah, the Three Graces. Dare I ask if your full name is Euphrosyne, Miss Grace?"

Rose was surprised. She had not thought to expect this level of erudition from a gentleman dressed as magnificently as Mr. Fotheringay–Phipps. Although, since he'd clearly understood her Greek, she shouldn't be surprised. "Why, yes, as a matter of fact, it is, but I have always been called Rose."

The smile that slowly spread over his face made Rose feel like giggling once more.

Rose folded her fan away and returned his smile. There was something different about this man. She could not put her finger on it, but somehow, despite his dandified appearance, she continued to feel the certain rush of understanding between them. In his company, the evening was so much nicer, more interesting.

"Have you been reading Greek mythology recently, Mr. Fotheringay–Phipps?" Rose asked.

"Fungy, please." Rose nodded, and Fungy continued smoothly, "Shouldn't be too interested in the classics, Miss Grace, nor, perhaps, speak the language publicly. It's completely understandable that you should know it, since your father is so well known in archaeological fields, but it is simply not the thing. *'The height of cleverness is being able to conceal it.'*"

"De La Rochefoucauld!" Rose's father exclaimed, quite pleased with himself for having known the source of the quote.

Rose wished she could be annoyed with Fungy for reprimanding her in public. But he had done it in such a pleasant way that she simply could do nothing but acquiesce.

"A young lady should know nothing of the classics, no matter who her father is," the duke huffed.

Rose immediately felt her hackles rise. She narrowed her eyes, ready to attack, when Fungy interceded. "Ah, but *a woman beautiful in mind as well as in form is a thing indeed to behold.*"

"Who said that?" Lord Pemberton–Howe asked, still caught up in the game of quotes.

Fungy gave him a brilliant smile. "I just did."

Rose nearly hit herself in the eye with her fan, as her hand flew up to her mouth to stifle her giggles. At a quick flick of her wrist, her fan opened and she used it to cover her mouth.

No one had ever said anything so sweet and charming to her! Perhaps this was going to be more fun than she had thought. Even her father looked amused.

"That is an unusual bracelet you are wearing, Miss Grace," Fungy said, holding his quizzing glass to his eye in order to get a better look at it.

"Thank you," Rose said, touching her bracelet. "It was my mother's."

"It is a coin from Macedonia. On its head is Artemis — or Diana, as the Romans called her..."

"Papa," Rose replaced her hand on her father's arm to stop his impromptu lecture before he began in earnest. "I don't think Fungy needs to hear the entire history of the coin."

"Oh, er, yes, of course."

"But perhaps some other time, my lord," Fungy said, politely.

They were quietly joined at that moment by a rather plain, brown–haired young woman. "Miss

Grace, have you met my daughter, Harriet?" Lord Halsbury asked.

"A pleasure to meet you," Rose said. Although she had been enjoying her conversation with Fungy, meeting another young woman her own age was just what she needed in order to put a foot forward in this strange society. And it would be nice to make a new friend.

※

Miss Halsbury was introduced to the other gentlemen, but instead of speaking with them, she turned to Rose and took a small step away from the gentlemen so that they could speak without disturbing them. "How are you enjoying your first party, Miss Grace?"

Rose looked at the other woman in amazement. "How did you know that this was my first party?"

"Oh, I was watching you earlier and you looked rather nervous, so I just assumed... But perhaps I'm wrong?"

"No. No, in fact, you are absolutely correct. Is it yours as well?" Rose asked, hoping that perhaps the other woman was in the same position as she.

"Oh, no. I am nearly one and twenty. I have been out for years," she said.

Rose nodded. She did suspect that that had been too much to hope for. "I'm the same age, but we've only just returned from Greece." .

She noticed Mr. Fotheringay–Phipps being beckoned to by Lord Halsbury, and watched him move away with a sinking heart. She had hoped that she'd get a chance to speak with him some more, but she supposed she should be happy to have Miss Halsbury to speak with, and perhaps Mr.— Fungy would come back

A Dandy In Disguise

and speak with her again after he was done speaking with Lord Halsbury.

"It must have been fascinating to live abroad," Miss Halsbury said, trying to reclaim Rose's attention.

Rose, however, was watching Fungy as Lord Halsbury spoke quietly into his ear and then handed him a card, which Fungy immediately slipped into his waistcoat pocket.

To her surprise, she felt an odd void, even as she stood speaking with Miss Halsbury in the midst of the crowded ballroom. Fungy had such an air about him, a vibrancy despite his outward appearance of boredom. Hopefully, he would return soon.

She turned back to Miss Halsbury. What had she asked? Oh yes, living abroad. "Yes, indeed, it was quite interesting, only... only I am afraid we never really had much in the way of society. My mother did her best to teach me how to go on in society, but I'm finding my social skills to be severely lacking. I do hope you will excuse me, and correct me, if I make any mistakes."

Sadly, when he was finished speaking with Lord Halsbury, Fungy moved even further away to speak with another young woman and her mama.

Miss Halsbury laughed lightly. "I am certain that you will do quite well, nonetheless," Miss Halsbury said. She, too, was keeping her eyes on Fungy, Rose noticed. She supposed he had the same effect on all young women.

"I hope so," Rose answered. "There seem to be so many things one needs to know in order to go on properly."

Rose watched as the girl he was speaking with smoothed down her dress in such a way that it looked as if Fungy had just complimented her on it.

She found herself smoothing down her own silk dress.

"Fashion is certainly one thing you do not need assistance with," Miss Halsbury said, eyeing her gown.

"Hmm? Oh, I don't know the first thing about what is fashionable and what is not. My sisters and I simply went to a modiste who told us precisely what to have made."

Luckily, the high-waisted style that appeared to be the fashion was flattering to her tall, slender form. Although Miss Halsbury was not precisely fat, she certainly could not be considered thin either. Her ample bosom seemed to be in danger of spilling out of the top of her dress. All of the flounces at the bottom of her gown gave the impression that she was rather short and squat, which, Rose realized as she stood next to the young woman, she really wasn't.

"Although," her new friend went on, "your gown is really cut much too high. A lower-cut bodice is much more the fashion."

Rose was certain she meant this in a friendly way. But still the remark made her feel rather self-conscious—perhaps she had erred in insisting that the modiste cut the dress more modestly.

"Er, yes, I know. I just couldn't see myself showing so much," Rose explained, awkwardly. It wasn't that she didn't have enough to show, it was just that she wasn't used to such a display.

Miss Halsbury gave her a sympathetic smile. "You will get used to it."

Fungy made the girl he was speaking with laugh, and then with a slight bow, moved on to charm the next young lady.

Rose swallowed back a sigh. He probably would not be back after all.

A Dandy In Disguise

"Rose, you must remember that we are no longer in Greece! I cannot comprehend how you could have been so rude. It is sad to say, but you must not assume that the people around you have the same level of intelligence as you are used to." Lord Pemberton–Howe said. He stood across from her, both hands leaning on the large mahogany table that dominated his study, littered with papers and correspondence as always. His coat and waistcoat were both unbuttoned and hanging open. If he leaned down just another inch, his silver buttons would probably thunk against the wood of his desk and remind him that he had not finished dressing properly.

Rose bowed her head. Her hands were clasped in front of her and she was biting the inside of her lip. Her father must have been truly upset about the previous night's incident. She had hoped that he would forget all about it, and he hadn't mentioned it immediately after they'd gotten home, but then she'd been called into the library first thing this morning.

She now absorbed his anger like a sponge, hoping that venting his annoyance would make him feel better so that her punishment wouldn't be too severe.

"You are right, Papa. I see now that I was wrong to have spoken as I did. I am sorry," she said, quietly. Perhaps a meek reply would help soften him. It usually did.

"I have never been so embarrassed. The Duke of Argyll, Rose! He is a strong supporter of the Archaeological Society and our work, as well as a well–respected member of the *ton*. You must watch your tongue. Surely your mother taught you how to behave properly in society?"

"Well, no, Papa. How could you ever think that she did? In fact, she told me that it would be best if I stayed away from society altogether. You know that she believed that it's no more than a market for girls to be sold off to the highest bidder—or for married ladies with titled husbands to prove their own importance to those lower on the social scale."

Lord Pemberton–Howe frowned at his daughter, but nodded reluctantly. He said nothing for a full minute, but stood running his hand through what little hair there was left on his head.

Rose felt a stab of concern, . He was looking very tired all of a sudden and. Rose was reminded of the fact that his well–being was now as much her responsibility as that of her two younger sisters.

It had been a hard year for them all. Ever since her mother had died, Rose had done her best to take on her role, and to live up to it, but it wasn't easy when all she'd ever had to worry about was her own interests. Rose was ashamed to admit that she mourned not only for her mother, but at times for herself as well.

"What is it, Papa?" she asked, scolding herself for even letting her mind wander into such selfish thoughts.

He shook his head and sat down heavily in his leather chair. "I'm afraid I cannot argue with what your mother taught you, but you still need to be more careful about how you behave in public. And, although I have no desire to sell you off, I..." he paused for a moment, looking pained. "Please, Rose, you must seriously look about you for a husband."

"What are you saying, Papa?" Rose sat down on the chair just behind her, her knees suddenly too weak to hold her up. Was caring for her father and sisters going to be the least of her worries, then? She lowered her gaze to the floor.

"You *know* that you need to find a husband, my dear."

"Well, yes, but I want to fall in love, just like you and Mama. I want a gentleman to court me, to read poems to me, to take me for moonlit walks." She refocused her eyes back onto her father. "I don't want to get married to just anyone. I want to marry a man I love, and who loves me with all of his heart and soul."

Her father gave her a sad smile. "I would wish all of those things for you, my dear, I would. But, unfortunately, we no longer have that luxury."

"I don't understand, Papa." Rose was glad she was sitting down, for she was beginning to feel oddly light-headed.

"I am sorry, my dear, but you need to marry. Quickly. We do not have the time for you to look for love. You need to marry someone with money, soon. I don't care for a title, but..." Her father let out a heart-felt sigh. "Our finances are stretched beyond their limits. We cannot continue in this fashion for much longer."

"But surely..." No, this could not be happening.

"No. There is nothing left." He shifted through the papers on his desk. "There is no money coming in from my estate, and I have already spent everything that your mother brought to our marriage on our last archaeological expedition. That's why we had to return so quickly. There was no money to finish the work. And now..."

He paused and picked up a sheaf of bills. Rose recognized them—they were from the mantua makers, the fabric stores and other shops where she and her sisters had purchased their new wardrobes.

"...now," her father continued, "we have all of these bills I cannot pay."

"Not at all?"

He shook his head sadly. "Not one, Rosebud. I simply do not have the money."

"How could there be no money from your estate, Papa? I thought you owned quite a lot of property."

Her father looked a little confused, but shook his head decisively. "I do. But according to these reports from my steward, it's just breaking even. There hasn't been any profit for many years now."

"And you trust your steward?" Rose had to ask.

"But of course I do! What a question, girl. Strate has been my steward for nearly fifteen years. He is as straight and honest as his name."

Rose nodded. It wasn't fair. It wasn't right for her father to ask this of her, her heart screamed out, no matter that her mind was telling her that she was truly their only hope. Her father wouldn't have asked this of her otherwise, she was certain. "But... how can I marry without love?" The words tumbled from her lips, by-passing her brain altogether.

She watched as he ran his fingers through his hair once again. Could he possibly look even more miserable than she felt?

Her father shrugged hopelessly. "It is what needs to be done. It is how most of society does it. You are our only hope now, Rose. Be a good girl and find a nice, wealthy man to marry. Quickly. I know you can do it."

Rose was silent. There was nothing she could say. Nothing she could do but what her father said Marry rich, marry soon.

A Dandy In Disguise

She stood up, feeling as if someone had placed a wooden beam across her shoulders. "I will do the best I can, Papa."

"I know you will. You're a good girl. I know I can count on you." He placed the offending bills into a drawer and shut them away.

Rose smiled wanly at this typical action by her father. Hiding them would not make them go away, but at least they wouldn't be staring him in the face.

And smiling and hiding were better alternatives than giving in to their true feelings.

Three

Upstairs in the drawing room, Rose's sisters were eagerly awaiting her verdict.

Laia was sitting with the stitching Great-aunt Farmington had forced on her, bright red head bowed over the frame. Thalia paced back and forth in front of the empty fireplace, long legs stretching out in front of her in the most unladylike way.

It was lucky that it was a warm spring and they had no need for fires, Rose thought. Considering their finances, they would probably not be able to afford the coal even if it were necessary.

Or their new clothes, she added to herself, admiring Laia's white-and-blue striped muslin dress and blue kid slippers, just the thing for a girl who would only be making her curtsey to society in another two years. Thalia's pale green dress, which came down only to just above her ankles, and brown kid half-boots were also exactly right for an active girl of fifteen. Both their dresses and shoes were new, and, along with her own new wardrobe, would be paid for dearly—as soon as Rose found a husband who wouldn't mind paying their bills.

"Well?" Thalia asked as soon as she noticed Rose standing in the doorway.

Laia set aside her work. "What did he say? Are you going to be punished?" she asked as if it were a treat.

A Dandy In Disguise

Rose came in and sat down on the sofa opposite Laia. "No. But I have to marry. Soon." She hesitated only long enough to tuck a stray brown curl back into the knot at the top of her head, and then related the news of their financial situation to her sisters. Just as her mother had, she kept nothing from them.

"You poor thing!" Laia exclaimed, sitting back against the sofa.

"Oh, but this will be fun!" Thalia said, standing still for the first time since Rose had come into the room. Her bright green eyes, just like her mother's and both of her sisters', sparkled with mischief.

Rose and Laia both turned to look incredulously at her.

"What do you mean, fun?" Rose asked.

"I mean *fun*." She scrunched up her forehead, adolescent brain clearly working hard. "We can look through all the gentlemen of the *ton* and pick one out for you. We'll have to find out who is rich, of course, and discount any who are not. And then we'll discard all the old ones, the ugly ones, and those who are not sportsmen—you can't marry a man who doesn't love sport, you know." Thalia paused for a breath.

"Thalia, you make this sound..." Rose began, but Laia, who was closer in age to Thalia, had caught on to her younger sister's excitement.

"Of course! What an excellent scheme! We'll go to Hyde Park this afternoon and begin our search. It shouldn't be too difficult. I'm certain you met quite a few gentlemen already last night, Rose."

"Well..."

"Oh come now, don't say that you don't remember their names!" Laia said, before thoughtfully poking her needle through her sampler. "I wonder how we will figure out who is wealthy enough?"

"We can look at their horses," Thalia suggested. "A man who is wealthy wouldn't buy a horse without fine points!" She threw her long dark brown braids over her shoulders and began to pace back and forth again, thinking this through.

"And what if he isn't a good judge of horseflesh?" Rose asked, trying hard not to laugh at her little sister.

"Well, then you definitely should *not* marry him," she said very seriously.

Rose lost control. Her laughter bubbled out of her. Her sisters were being utterly ridiculous!

"And he should be very handsome. Don't forget that, Thalia. Rose cannot marry a man who is not pleasing to the eye. I think one like those in the friezes Papa found in Greece, with a well–sculpted chest and arms."

Rose wiped tears of laughter from her eyes. "Oh, yes, definitely. But then, perhaps, I should marry a Greek?"

"But we are not in Greece any more, and surely there have got to be some men like that here."

"Shall I ask the gentleman you choose to disrobe, so that I may see his muscles before I marry him?" Rose joked.

Thalia smiled, clearly pleased with the idea, but Laia looked horrified. "You can't ask a gentleman to bare himself!"

"Oh? But I should be sure that he is wealthy, engages in sports, and should judge him by the horse he rides, yes?"

"That's right!" Thalia said.

"Well..." Laia was beginning to look uncertain. "Tell us who you met last night, then, Rose. Were there any interesting or eligible gentlemen at the ball?"

Rose became serious, thinking back to the previous evening.

"Well, I met your Mr. Haston, Laia, but I don't think he is right for me."

"I thought he was very sweet," Laia said, defending the gentleman.

"Sweet, yes. Intelligent? No."

"Oh well, now you really are becoming quite particular."

"You want him to be smart as well as a sportsman? I don't know, Rose." Even Thalia sounded dubious about finding a gentleman imbued with both of those qualities.

Rose nodded. "Yes, he definitely has to be intelligent. And it would be nice if he had a good sense of humor."

Thalia and Laia had to agree with that.

"And while we're building castles in the air," Rose continued, enjoying herself, "I think he should be an archeologist like Papa. That would truly be wonderful."
"And he should be romantic," Laia sighed.

"You two are so ridiculous." Thalia scowled at them both. "There is no gentleman who is wealthy, a sportsman, has a good sense of humor, is handsome, an archaeologist *and* romantic!" She ticked off all of the qualities on her fingers. "You might as well give it up right now."

Rose sat back and frowned. Thalia was right. There was no man who would fit that description.

"But she *has* to marry," Laia complained.

Rose sighed. "Well, I suppose I shall just have to give something up. But let's not worry about that now. Let's see first who my choices are."

"Were there no other interesting gentlemen, Rose?" Thalia asked.

"Only one other," Rose said, feeling her face grow warm as she remembered Mr. Fotheringay–Phipps. He was very handsome, and he made her laugh.

"By the look on your face, I would say this one was very interesting!" Laia exclaimed.

"Well, there was one gentleman who was quite... *interesting*," Rose admitted, feeling an unbidden smile creep onto her lips. "His name is Mr. Fotheringay–Phipps, but he is called Fungy."

"Fungy?" Thalia repeated, making a face.

Laia frowned. "What sort of name is Fungy?"

"He sounds like a mushroom. Is he?" Thalia asked.

Rose laughed. "No, he is not a mushroom."

"Does he have a big flat head and a tall thin body?" Laia asked, laughing.

"No! Although he is tall, and rather thin. He seemed well–muscled actually, and looked like he might be a sportsman. But he wore the most ridiculous high collar and an absolutely dazzling waistcoat. Frankly, he looked as if he might be a dandy."

She turned to Thalia, "And, no, my dearest, I do *not* know what sort of horse he rides, for we were at a soirée and I didn't see him arrive or leave."

"Did you ask him what sports he played?" she asked.

"No, I didn't. If you meet him, you may do so."

"So, he is handsome?" Laia interrupted.

"Yes, tolerably so. He has blond hair, a well–sculpted face, and beautiful blue eyes."

"And is he wealthy?" she asked, letting her stitching fall to her lap.

A Dandy In Disguise

"That I don't know," Rose admitted.

"But wouldn't it be wonderful if he was?" Laia sighed. "He could be the one—although he does have a rather unfortunate name."

"Well, she can't marry him until *we* meet him and approve, that's for certain." Thalia crossed her arms in front of her.

Both Rose and Laia broke out laughing at her serious demeanor. After wiping the tears from her eyes, Rose said, "I assure you, I will marry no one without your approval, Miss Thalia."

Thalia nodded her head regally, and then skipped out of the room.

When they had caught their breath from laughing, Laia said seriously, "Truly, Rose, who *will* you marry?"

Rose sobered up immediately. "I don't know, Laia, but I know that I need to find someone quickly. And if his wealth is all he has to offer, I may need to accept that—for all our sakes."

Fungy paused on the landing just outside of the drawing room as the voice of his good friend Sinclair Stratton, Viscount Reath seeped from under the closed door. "You know I would be honored to be the baby's godfather, Merry, but what about Fungy?" He'd not meant to eavesdrop, but as Merry's cousin he was a frequent visitor and it was customary for him not to be announced by the Marquis' lofty butler. Inadvertently, he'd almost walked in on this most intriguing conversation.

"Honestly, I'm not sure that he's responsible enough. When it comes to dressing the baby, you know Fungy will be the first person we call. But this is a very important position—and Teresa and I don't want to entrust it to someone who may make a mockery of it. We know that you will take it seriously. We can trust you." Merry's voice was quiet but firm.

Fungy felt a weight settle in his chest.

Sin sighed. "I appreciate that, and of course I will be happy to do my best for your son. But when it comes time to release him out into the world..."

"Absolutely, Fungy is my man," Merry finished with a laugh. "But until then, Sin, and in everything else, we're counting on you."

Fungy looked down at his immaculate ensemble. Was this all he was valued for—dressing properly?

"And, naturally, Fungy will be able to introduce him to all the right people. Amazing the number of people he knows and socializes with," Sin said, still defending him.

"Indeed. He manages to meet and befriend all sorts. But have you once seen him actually doing anything beyond being social and giving his precious fashion advice?"

Sin laughed, giving in. "I must admit that I can't imagine Fungy doing anything actually worthwhile."

"No, neither can I. Don't really think the old boy has it in him," Merry agreed with a chuckle.

Fungy felt the heaviness inside of him blossom into outright pain as these words sliced through his chest. He couldn't take any more of this. He turned and was about to descend the stairs once more when Julian Ritchie, Lord Huntley, came bounding up.

"Ah, Fungy! Thought I'd run into you here," he said, slapping Fungy on the back and propelling him toward the drawing room.

Julian had strongly taken to dressing fashionably ever since he'd moved to England from his native

A Dandy In Disguise

Calcutta, bonding with Fungy as a mentor and guide in all things fashionable. Now, despite his mixed heritage, he always managed to look more impeccably English than anyone. It was really quite easy at times to completely forget that he wasn't entirely English.

Fungy hesitated, desperate to escape. But he had no choice. He squared his shoulders, and entered the room with Julian.

Four

Fungy saw Sin look quickly away from the door as he entered the room with Julian. Pushing a lock of his straight jet–black hair off his broad forehead, Sin helped himself to a cup of coffee, his slashing eyebrows pulled low over his eyes. Fungy had no particular desire to meet his eyes either.

Merry, on the other hand, was looking very relaxed on a sofa with a sleeping baby in his lap. His coat of blue superfine and pale yellow pantaloons were covered with a soft blanket to protect the baby from the buttons (or perhaps the other way around). The baby, clearly taking after his father with his fair skin and blond hair, looked rather angelic in his sleep—more like a cherub than the squalling little creature his cousin had described to him two weeks ago, just after the child was born.

But that explained the smell in the room. It definitely smelled of baby—and coffee, he thought as he watched Julian head directly over to the sideboard for a cup.

"Morning, Sin," Julian said in his normal hearty voice. Then, noticing the baby as he passed, he dropped his voice to a whisper. "Morning, Merry."

"It's all right," Merry assured him. "I don't think anything could wake him when he's sleeping."

"Oh. Then why are you watching him?" Julian asked, helping himself to a slice of the cake as well.

A Dandy In Disguise

"Teresa's asleep, and she still hasn't found a nursemaid she is happy with." Merry shifted a little under the weight of the sleeping baby. "She had best do so soon, however. Neither of us is getting much sleep because of this little one. He was up half the night wanting to be fed, changed, burped, and goodness only knows what else. Teresa is running herself ragged, and I can't sleep with all the commotion."

"What you get for procreating," Fungy said, straining to make his voice as light as always. He was having a hard time putting Sin and Merry's disloyal words from his mind.

Sin laughed. "Not something you need to worry about anytime soon, Fungy."

Fungy moved to help himself to some coffee as well, although wishing for something stronger. "I'll leave that to you three."

"Why *don't* you get married, Fungy? It's a rather pleasant state to live in," Julian said, before taking a large bite of his cake.

"I had a rather unfortunate experience with love some time ago. Rather not repeat it."

Merry sat up. "You still think about that? My God, that must have been at least ten years ago."

"Fifteen, actually," Fungy corrected.

"What happened?" Julian asked. He widened his odd turquoise-colored eyes, making them stand out even more from his honey brown face.

"Fell in love. The lady married someone else. She moved to America and took my heart with her," Fungy answered succinctly, not wanting to dwell on the subject any longer than necessary.

Julian shook his head sadly. "Love is a damned tricky business."

"Indeed."

"But, really, Fungy, don't you think it's time you put that aside and settled down?" Merry asked.

"How about an occupation?" Sin asked, settling his large frame into a delicate chair, since Merry seemed to be taking up the entire sofa himself. "I found serving as a diplomat in India to be great fun, and it put me right in the mood to marry once I returned."

Fungy gave Sin a little smile. He was a good friend, unlike some, he thought, leveling his gaze at Merry. "Thank you, all the same, Sin, quite happy with the way things are."

He then turned fully to Merry. "No need to dredge the old heart up out of the muck and mire. If and when I feel the need to set up my nursery, I'll find someone who will not try to, er, engage my finer sensibilities."

Merry just looked at him sadly. Turning to his other friends, Fungy noticed that they too seemed to be regarding him with rather sober expressions on their faces.

"No need to be so glum, old chums! Just because you have all succeeded in filling your hearts with joy, doesn't mean that I need to. Quite happy the way I am, truly."

"It's just a shame, that's all," Sin said.

"Really should try it, Fungy, marriage is..."

"My goodness, look at the time!" Fungy said, interrupting Julian. "I've got an appointment. Frightfully sorry and all that, got to run." He made for the door as quickly as he could.

If there was one thing he could not stand, it was people feeling sorry for him—and especially not his closest friends.

A Dandy In Disguise

He was quite happy with his life just the way it was, just as he had told them. There was nothing that he would change, not for an instant, so there was no use even wasting the time thinking about it.

What had hurt him, however, was the fact that Merry and Sin, who had known him for most of his life, seemed to have forgotten what his social mask hid. Was it possible that he had forgotten as well?

He had to admit that his run–in the other evening with Miss Grace had sparked something inside of him. It was just a flicker of a reminiscence—of reading and discussing classic texts with his peers at university, of playing with the meanings in the complicated texts they pored over all day and into the night. How long had it been since he'd picked up Plato or Homer or even one of the lighter plays by Euripides, which he used to enjoy so much?

How long had it been since he had truly engaged his mind?

He'd completely given up his passion for the classics long ago, but Miss Grace had made him recall those sweet days of his youth.

And something else as well—a feeling deep within him, long buried—the heat of attraction to a beautiful woman.

"Thank you for the dance, my lord," Rose said, curtsying to the gentleman as he returned her to her great–aunt.

The gentleman bent his tall, thin frame in her direction and then loped off to find his next partner.

"Well, he seems to be a very nice young man, Rose, and I hear he's got ten thousand a year," Aunt Farmington said quietly.

"Yes," Rose replied with a frown.. It would be nice, however, if he had a brain to go with all that money."

Aunt Farmington glared at Rose. "You are entirely too fastidious, my girl. You are supposed to be searching for a wealthy husband, not the man of your dreams."

Rose sighed. It was true. As her father had said, she did not have the luxury of waiting to find the perfect man or of giving him time to woo her properly.

"I know. I only wish I could find someone a little closer to my dream than Lord Simpleton, or whatever his name was."

Her aunt chuckled. "Stiplton, I believe... er, something like that."

Rose couldn't help but laugh, too. Clearly the gentleman hadn't left a great impression on her aunt either.

She sobered up quickly enough as she saw Lady Farmington narrow her eyes at another rather fatuous–looking young man.

"I had always thought that I would marry a man who simply took my breath away, the way Mama said Papa did to her the first time they met."

Lady Farmington snapped her head back to peer at Rose, her already wrinkled forehead crinkling further with concern.

"And then he would bring me flowers and write poems to my eyes or some such thing," Rose added softly, thinking wistfully of the dreams she and her sisters had concocted yesterday.

"One would think that a girl as intelligent as you would be beyond dreaming of romantic nonsense like that," her aunt said caustically.

A Dandy In Disguise

Rose studied the fan in her hands for a moment and then gave a little shrug. "It is silly, I suppose," she said, having to quickly blink to take the stinging from her eyes. "And it has nothing to do with my current life."

She lifted her chin and placed a smile on her lips. "Are there any other eligible young men to whom you could introduce me?"

Her aunt looked at her silently for a moment, blinking her watery hazel eyes, and shook her head. All of a sudden, though, her face brightened. A rather uncharacteristic smile twitched onto her lips, and she walked slowly over to another older lady behind Rose, who sat in a gilt chair facing the dance floor, her tall feathered turban slowly nodding in time to the sound of the musicians fine–tuning their instruments.

"Mrs. Saxton, how very pleasant to see you again!"

The other lady looked up. "Why, Lady Farmington, what a very pleasant surprise. It has been such a long time since we've had a chat. Do join me."

Lady Farmington took the empty seat next to her and then motioned to Rose.

"My dear, your father is just over there. Why don't you converse with him for a little while? Perhaps he has a young man to introduce to you."

Rose turned to see her father standing by himself next to the entrance to the card room. Turning back to her aunt, she saw that it would now be completely useless to do anything but what she had suggested, for the lady was engaged in deep conversation with her friend.

"Aunt Farmington has abandoned me in favor of a gossip with one of her friends," Rose informed her father, walking over to join him.

"What? But..."

"Do not worry, Papa, we are merely taking a little break from husband–hunting." Rose sighed heavily. "I am so tired of dancing and being pleasant."

Her father gave a little chuckle. "I must say, I don't believe I've ever seen you behave so well for such a long period of time."

Rose turned to her father, a smile tugging up one corner of her mouth. "What shall we do, Papa? Is there someplace more interesting where we could go?"

Lord Pemberton–Howe raised his eyebrows in mock surprise. "Euphrosyne, you aren't suggesting that I take my own daughter…"

"Oh, all right, how about just into the card room, then? Surely that can't be so bad."

Her father turned and looked a little longingly into that room. He had been planning on slipping in there himself, Rose was sure of it.

She took his arm and gave him a little pull in that direction.

"No, no, my dear, it is not done," he protested.

"What is not done?" Rose feigned ignorance.

"Young girls do not play cards at balls. You should be out here dancing with all the young bucks."

"But I am tired of dancing, Papa. Come, it can't be wrong if I am with you." Rose gave him a sweet, pleading smile, and saw him begin to relent.

"All right, but just for a short time, then back to your dancing."

Rose tucked her hand into the crook of his elbow. "Perhaps there will be some eligible young men in there you could introduce to me."

Five

The air in the card room was hazy with cigar smoke. Rose swallowed hard, trying not to cough.

Her father paused to survey the room for a place for them to sit down. Rose could hardly see anything; somehow, there just weren't enough candles to light the room very well. She wondered if that was intentional, so that people couldn't see their cards or how much money they'd won — or lost.

The room was filled mostly with men, with only a few ladies there as well, playing cards and chatting. Rose didn't mind being one of the few women present — she was used to it, after being raised at an archaeological dig.

Her father led her to a table where two young men were sitting idly chatting and shuffling a deck of cards.

The two gentlemen immediately stood up as Rose moved toward the table.

"Pemberton–Howe," her father said, holding out his hand to the first of the two gentlemen. "And my daughter, Miss Rose Grace."

"Jack Aiken," a rather ordinary–looking gentleman answered, shaking her father's hand. His was long and thin, as was everything about him. His long face was accentuated by a very long and thin nose. His eyes were small and his hair, which was long and straight, drooped into them. Rose was not at all impressed by his looks, and slightly disconcerted by his deep voice, which was like an ominous roll of thunder from far away.

"This is Lord Kirtland," Mr. Aiken added, pointing to the gentleman next to him.

In sharp contrast to his companion, *this* gentleman was just the sort to put a girl in mind of marriage and romance. Although not very tall, he was well–built in such a way that Rose could imagine that he might look just like the Greek statues she and her sisters had admired. He was slim, but with powerful–looking, broad shoulders, and muscular legs. His finely chiseled chin was strong and masculine and he had brown, almost black eyes. Rose did her best not to stare, managing to give both men a curtsey.

"Kirtland? I believe we may have met before," Lord Pemberton–Howe said, shaking his hand.

"Yes sir, at an Archaeological Society meeting. I spoke to you last week after your speech on the ruins of Athens."

"Ah, yes, yes. I remember now." Lord Pemberton–Howe smiled and sat down.

"You are an archeologist, my lord?" Rose asked, moving around the table to the other empty chair. Could this be? Could she be so lucky as to have found a handsome archeologist? She was never so glad to have convinced her father to bring her into this room.

Now if he was rich and unmarried, she would truly be in luck. And after the dismal time she'd had so far this evening, it was about time that she met someone promising.

"Just a hobby, Miss Grace, although I hope someday to make it my occupation. But as yet, I have not had the opportunity to do so."

His dark eyes peered deeply into her own as if he were sizing up her soul. A shiver ran up her spine. There

A Dandy In Disguise

was something different, something exciting—something dangerous about this man. She sat down abruptly.

Lord Kirtland shuffled the deck of cards in front of him, a small smile playing on his lips. "Would you be interested in a game of whist, Miss Grace?" he asked his voice soft and smooth.

Rose firmly pulled herself together. "I would enjoy that, I'm certain, only... I don't know how to play. Would you be so kind as to teach me the game?" She tried fluttering her eyelashes at him a bit as she'd seen other young women do, and was rewarded with a broad smile.

"I would be honored. Aiken, you will be patient for a few moments while I teach Miss Grace the basics?"

"Of course, by all means." Mr. Aiken gave her a small smile and then turned to engage her father in conversation.

The game was simple enough to learn. Everyone placed a card on the table and the highest or the trump card won the trick. They tried playing a few hands just so that she could catch on. When she pronounced herself ready, they added wagering to the game, starting off small, at a penny a point.

Her father was not a very shrewd player. He tended to lose track of which cards had already been played, and at one point even forgot which was the trump. Lord Kirtland, however, was an excellent player, and Rose enjoyed matching her wits with his.

After their second hand, Mr. Haston, whom Rose had first met during her uncomfortable interlude with the Duke of Argyll, strolled up to their table. "Ah, my lord, Miss Grace. Pleasant to see you again."

Rose looked up. "Oh, Mr. Haston, how do you do? Would you care to join us?"

"No, thank you. Ain't... ain't room at the table," he said, with a small pout that he quickly exchanged for an polite smile.

"Er, please, take my seat," her father said, standing up. "Not very good at this."

"Oh yes, please do take my father's place," Rose begged him sweetly. She was certain she would do much better if she had a different partner than her father.

"Don't mind, sir?" Haston said, sitting down. Her father indicated that he did not, and began to let his eyes wander around the room, looking at some of the other games being played.

The next hand was dealt and Rose was happy to find that Mr. Haston was a better player, although he tended as well to become distracted and make silly mistakes.

As the game went on, the stakes were raised. With a slightly more skilled partner and growing confidence, Rose did not object. She was surprised, and quite pleased, to notice that the pile of coins that sat in front of her was growing, rather than shrinking. Although she could hear the music playing in the other room, she was very happy to push out of her mind her whole reason for being present at the ball.

She eventually had so many coins in front of her that she wasn't exactly sure what to do with them. With an embarrassed giggle, she simply opened her reticule and let them all slide in.

"You know what this reminds me of, Aiken," Lord Kirtland said, laughing a bit, "that time I won a monkey from old Burncaster and he paid me in coin."

Mr. Aiken gave a small crooked smile, but said nothing.

Rose, however, stopped what she was doing. "You won a monkey? Whatever did you do with it?"

The gentlemen began to laugh. "Not a real monkey, Miss Grace," Mr. Haston said.

"A monkey is five hundred pounds," Lord Kirtland explained.

"Oh! My goodness, what a lot of money!"

Lord Kirtland shrugged noncommittally.

"What would you have done if you had lost?" Rose could not help asking.

"It wouldn't have been a problem, Miss Grace," Lord Kirtland said, giving her a little smile.

"Not for Kirtland," Mr. Aiken added.

"Oh." Rose could say nothing more. The thought of winning or losing that much money was rather overwhelming.

But then she caught her father's eye. It was clear that he was thinking the same as her. While he, too, was rather shocked at Lord Kirtland's cavalier attitude toward money, that meant only one thing—Rose had to find out if Lord Kirtland was unmarried.

Things were beginning to look better and better.

And they looked even better later that night when Rose had counted all of the money she had won that evening at cards. She had nearly thirty pounds! That was going to be a good start on paying the bills that still sat in her father's desk drawer.

She could barely contain her giggles. What a lot of money to have won!

She sat back on her bed, rearranging her shawl around her shoulders and her shift over her slightly chilled feet, and thought about the evening. Lord

Kirtland seemed almost too good to be true. He was an archeologist, apparently a wealthy one, and rather handsome besides. A few discreet questions by her father had led them to the conclusion that Lord Kirtland was, in fact, unmarried and might very well be interested in changing that in the near future.

There really wasn't much more that Rose could ask for in a husband.

Except, perhaps, love, her rebellious mind called out.

She shook off that thought. She didn't have that luxury. She needed to marry quickly, see their bills paid and her sisters taken care of.

Idly running her fingers through the pile of coins, she wondered if she could find a way to play cards again...

Rose sat up.

That was it! If she could win money playing cards—enough to pay their bills—then there would be no reason to rush into marriage, would there? And if there weren't the immediate problem of their bills, then perhaps she *could* take a little more time to fall in love. At the very least she could have a little romance.

She wondered if Lord Kirtland was a romantic man.

Six

Fungy had nearly reached the docks when he heard a female scream.

He stopped. These wharfs were no place for a woman. There were all sorts of ruffians around here who wouldn't think twice of taking advantage of a lady alone.

"Help! Oh, Thalia, swim! Please try and swim!" a vaguely familiar voice called out from not too far away.

Fungy took off running along the road next to the Thames towards the sound. Only a short distance away, two women stood at the edge of the dock, looking out into the ever-crowded water. Ships of all sizes, from large cargo ships to small sailing vessels to even smaller punting boats, warred with each other for space near the dock, some nearly coming close enough to touch.

Fungy had stepped up to offer his assistance to the two ladies, when he recognized one as Miss Grace. She stood clutching the arm of another young lady, as slender as she but with wild red hair escaping from a neat little hat.

The two were looking down into the water. Fungy followed their gaze into the choppy, muddy water of the river. For a moment, he saw nothing but a lady's hat, but a second later a dark head bobbed up to the surface.

"I... I'm caught on something!" the girl in the water gasped out before slipping under again.

A few sailors stopped what they were doing to gawp, but no one made a move to go in after the girl.

With so many ships anchored, there was a maze of ropes crisscrossing each other in a tangled mess. It was probably in these lines that the young lady had gotten caught.

Fungy looked down at his beautifully polished white–topped Hessian boots and buckskin breeches. He had worn his favorite blue coat and his pale yellow waistcoat with the blue flowers embroidered all over it.

With a sigh, he pulled off his boots, coat, and waistcoat. Then, with a clean move, he dove into the freezing cold, filthy water.

Fungy had always been a strong swimmer. Now he used his arms to carry him to where he had seen the girl surface. The water was so murky, however, that it was difficult to see much of anything underneath.

Taking a deep breath, he dove under. He grasped around and made contact with something slippery and slimy, recoiling instantly. He didn't even want to think of what it might be. No luck; he changed direction, swimming further out into the river. An enormous ship shifted closer to him and he quickly moved out of its way.

Fungy resurfaced and trod water as he thought. She hadn't been quite so close to the ships.

But he had to find her soon—before it was too late to save her.

A shout from the dock. "To your left, Fungy, to your left!"

Once again, he turned and searched in the other direction. To his relief, he saw a dark, wet head popping up not too far away. The girl sputtered out water, trying to take in deep breaths of air.

A Dandy In Disguise

"Miss!" Fungy called out—but she had gone under again.

He took another deep breath and dove under the water, reaching out in front of him. Finally, his hand touched something warm. It shifted away from him, but he grasped it firmly and swam upward. His head and hers came up out of the water at the same time.

"It's all right, I have you," he said as soon as he could regain his breath. The girl's wide green eyes took him in.

"I wasn't drowning. I'm stuck. My dress is caught on something and I can't tear it away," she said, gasping for breath. "I'm actually an excellent swimmer," she added.

"Well, I'm very glad to hear that. I would suggest, however, that you pick a more secluded spot the next time you decide to go bathing. Or better yet, a private lake in the countryside."

The girl surprised him by laughing breathlessly. "Thank you, sir, I do believe I shall take your advice. However, I must tell you that I did not intend to go swimming at all this afternoon. I fell in."

"Ah, well, that's a relief. This part of the Thames is not the most ideal for this sort of activity. Now let's see what we can do to set you free. I don't like all these ships and lines about."

With that, he dove back under the water. Through the darkness, he could see that her white dress was indeed caught on something among all of the ropes which crossed each other deep under the water. She had managed to tear the hem somewhat, so that it hung down lower than the rest of her dress, but it still held her firmly in place. With just another good strong tug it should tear free.

Fungy gave it a try—and indeed the dress came loose. He could feel the churning of the water as she kicked and swam off in the direction of the dock.

Fungy made a move to do the same, but found his own foot caught among the lines. He twisted and pulled, but the ropes only seemed to get tighter the more he struggled.

He was beginning to get desperate for air.

With a great deal of effort, he attempted to calm himself. He concentrated on not moving, when, completely unbidden, a thought came to the forefront of his mind—*really, old man, what have you got to lose?*

Fungy stopped struggling immediately and instead grappled with this thought. What did he have to lose?

He had no family, aside from his parents, whom he hadn't seen or heard from in months. And, of course, there was his cousin, Merry, who had turned on him only days before saying that he was feckless and irresponsible. He had no wife, no children... who would miss him if he died?

No one.

He had done nothing with his life and had left no legacy. There wasn't even a neckcloth knot or a style of waistcoat named after him.

It would be no great loss to the world if St. John Fotheringay–Phipps was no longer a part of it. He supposed he would be missed momentarily by a few people, but likely as not he would be forgotten with the next day's news.

Fungy felt the ropes that held his leg loosen. The shifting of the water and the ships above, along with the fact that he had stopped struggling, had freed his foot.

A Dandy In Disguise

But did he really want to swim up? Wouldn't it be just as well if he stayed here and drowned?

His lungs were beginning to ache with the need for air.

In the end, it was his natural instinct for survival that made him kick his legs. Within moments, his head broke through the surface of the water. He gasped in the warm air, but his mind was still lured by the deep. His heart and emotions warred within him. The shooting pain and an utter and thorough sadness were enough to pull him down below the surface once again—but a voice was calling out to him.

Such a sweet voice it was. One filled with fear and pleading. "Fungy! Mr. Fotheringay–Phipps! Oh, thank God, are you all right? Oh, please answer. Fungy!"

Miss Grace was on her hands and knees at the edge of the dock, leaning over toward the water. Near her was a ladder, at the top of which sat her two sisters. A crowd of onlookers was gathered nearby. A few sailors were peering into the water, but none seemed eager to jump in to save him.

Really, who could blame them?

With Rose Grace's lovely face hovering above him, all thoughts of drowning seeped out of Fungy's mind. He swam as best as he could to the ladder and slowly climbed up. Strong hands reached out and got hold of him, pulling him to safety.

His limbs felt like lead weights. If it were not for the help of the sailors, he was not certain he could have made it up entirely by himself. He was let down on to the ground next to the two ladies, evidently Miss Laia and Miss Thalia Grace.

He had the most horrendous taste in his mouth from the dirty water. He leaned over and spat back into the water, and tried to wipe his face dry with his soaking wet handkerchief.

"Oh please, Mr. Foth... Fungy, use mine. It is not much drier, but a bit cleaner at any rate." Miss Grace said, handing him the little scrap of cotton and lace that constituted her handkerchief.

It was clear to see that she must have recently been holding on to her recovering sister who Fungy had just saved. The whole front of her sprig muslin dress was soaked through, making the cotton cling quite indecently to her body. Even in exhaustion, Fungy could not help but admire the beautiful Miss Rose Grace.

He glanced from the youngest sister, with her rounded, child–like face and dark brown braids, now soaking wet and dripping; to the middle sister, the utter opposite with sharp, high cheekbones, a thin straight nose and those bright red curls; to Rose, who outshone both of her sisters, with features which highlighted the best of both of her sisters. Her face was not too thin, but pleasantly formed; her hair neither too red, nor too brown, but a beautiful auburn somewhere in between. Yes, she was definitely an angel come down to Earth to entice him into thinking distinctly devilish thoughts.

She handed him his coat and boots, but he immediately returned his coat. "Your sister might need this more than I," he said.

"Thank you, but someone has just gone to fetch a blanket for her from a nearby tavern," Miss Grace said, awkwardly holding onto his coat.

"Well, then, I believe you should wear it. The front of your dress is rather wet."

Miss Grace looked down at herself. Her face turned redder than her sister's hair, and she quickly slipped her arms into his coat and wrapped it around herself.

A Dandy In Disguise

Fungy nodded. That would help keep his mind from roaming where it shouldn't.

Knowing he would ruin his boots if he tried to put them on, he placed them by his side while he caught his breath.

"All roight then, guv'na?" a sailor asked him, leaning his foul-smelling mouth close to Fungy.

Knowing he did not smell too much better after his dip in the water, Fungy forced himself not to recoil. "Yes, thank you. I'll be all right."

"I cannot thank you enough, sir," Miss Grace began, but Fungy held up a hand to stop her gratitude.

"It is quite all right, Miss Grace. Do not say another word." With great effort—and a little assistance from Miss Grace and the sailor—he managed to stand up.

The weight of his wet clothes pulled at him, as did the exhaustion that made it difficult for him to move at all. But slowly, he managed to get his limbs moving and walked off, carrying his boots in his hand, to find a hackney to take him home.

"Fungy, please allow us..." Miss Grace called after him, but he just walked on, ignoring her. He could not contemplate being social just now, not even with a grateful lady as lovely as Miss Grace.

His mind was filled with all that had just happened, and especially the sobering feelings he had had while caught under the water. He was wet and tired, and it took all of his remaining strength to stay upright. He just wanted to get home.

But most importantly, he wanted to deal with the emotional drain of nearly drowning—on purpose.

Seven

Rose's heart was still pounding in her chest. Luckily, she didn't think anyone had noticed the tears she'd had to wipe off her cheeks more than once.

First Thalia had nearly drowned in that horrible river, and then Fungy had not surfaced for the longest time. She would not have been able to bear it, had anything happened to him while he was saving her sister.

She turned on Thalia, who now sat huddled, shivering, under a rough wool blanket on the ground. She knelt down in front of her and started to vigorously rub Thalia's arms to warm her, her worry venting itself in a burning anger she was having a hard time controlling.

"How could you, Thalia? I have never been so embarrassed in all my life! I can't believe you fell in. If you ever do anything like that again, I swear, I will see that you are punished so severely…"

"Rose!" Laia exclaimed, moving to sit up on her knees.

"But it was an accident." Thalia protested at the same time.

"It was an entirely avoidable accident," Rose said, looking around to make sure there was no one eavesdropping on their conversation. Luckily, this area of the dock was mostly empty, the officers and sailors from the ship moored nearby having all left.

A Dandy In Disguise

"No, don't you defend her either, Laia, because this is equally your fault," Rose said, turning back to her sisters. "I saw the way the two of you were fooling around, jumping in front of each other while I was trying to get information about the ship bringing our things from Greece."

Laia and Thalia sat quietly, looking at her from under their eyelashes. They both looked so contrite that for just a moment Rose felt her heart softening. But she quickly snapped back to the reality of the situation.

"Don't look at me like that. I know full well what you are doing and I am not Papa to be fooled by your sorrowful eyes. I taught you that trick, so it is not going to work with me."

"But Rose, it truly was an accident," Thalia complained. "I assure you, I had no intention of falling into that disgusting water."

Rose frowned and looked at the swirling brown water of the Thames next to them. It *was* truly disgusting. "No, I am certain that you did not. However, if you two hadn't been playing your silly game, whatever it was, then none of this would have happened."

"But it wasn't a silly game," Laia said.

"Well, Laia was trying to get a look at the sailors..." Thalia started.

"The officers," Laia interrupted.

"All right, the officers, on that ship and I was trying to stop her. You and Mama have said in the past that she shouldn't ogle men."

Rose looked incredulously to Laia, who had the grace to blush.

"Well, I..."

"I don't want to hear any more of this. Laia, I think you will be staying at home for the next three days until you learn to control yourself."

"But, Rose!" Laia objected.

"Not another word or else I will tell Papa what has occurred and let you see what sort of punishment he thinks is appropriate."

Laia opened and closed her mouth a few times, finally settling on a pout.

"I don't see why you're so angry, Rose," Thalia said quietly. "There was no harm done, if you don't count the loss of my hat and this dress—I didn't particularly like this dress anyway."

"What do you mean, no harm done!" Rose nearly shouted, jumping to her feet. "What about Fungy? What about the fact that both you and he nearly drowned? You didn't see how long he was under the water after he tore your dress free. I thought he was never going to come up again."

Laia and Thalia both looked at Rose in great surprise.

She swallowed the sob that tried to break free from her throat. "He nearly drowned, saving you, Thalia," she said hastily, wiping the tears from her cheeks.

"Rose, I am so sorry," Thalia said quietly. "I didn't know."

"You really like him." It was more of a statement than a question, but Laia was looking at her with wide eyes.

Rose felt her face grow hot. "No! I mean, well, I don't know the man, do I? We've only met once. But he was very kind to me when I met him and he got me out of an awkward situation. And now he has risked his life to save Thalia." She crossed her arms over her chest.

A Dandy In Disguise

The feeling of the soft wool of Fungy's coat under her fists let her imagine, for just a moment, that Fungy himself was enveloping her in his warmth.

Her sisters just looked at her, almost as if they were trying to read her mind. She turned away; she didn't know herself what the strange feelings running through were.

"Come, let's see if we can't find a hackney to take us home."

After all, she had decided just the previous night that Lord Kirtland was the most eligible man she had yet met. She could never marry a dandy, and she had no idea what his financial situation was. No, she should put all these odd thoughts of Fungy directly out of her mind.

But his torso and arms had looked truly magnificent in his nearly transparent wet shirt. There would be no need to ask him to bare himself for her to inspect his muscles. He had practically done so already.

The girls were silent for most of the ride back to their rented house on Soho Square. The hackney was dirty, and stank—or perhaps that was Thalia. Rose couldn't tell the difference. But it was not an altogether pleasant ride, despite opened windows.

"Why do you think he left so quickly?" Thalia asked.

Rose just looked at her, amazed that her sister should be thinking exactly the same thing that had been going through her own mind. She swallowed hard and shook her head. "I don't know."

"He seemed rather rude," Laia put in, clearly thinking along the same lines. "I mean, I know he had just saved Thalia's life, but you would think that he would have done the gentlemanly thing of seeing us home, or at the very least into a hackney to take us home."

"I suspect he was just cold and tired," Rose said, although she didn't know why she defended him. It was true that he had been a bit rude. Perhaps it was a good thing she had settled on Lord Kirtland.

They arrived home just then, so Rose was spared thinking about this any further.

"Miss Thalia! Miss Grace! What happened to you?" Reynolds, the Graces' butler, exclaimed loudly as they came into the house.

Three hands went up. "Shhh! Papa will hear!" they whispered fiercely.

But it was too late. Lord Pemberton–Howe threw open the library door before they could even move toward the stairs.

"What is this? What has occurred?"

"Nothing, Papa," Laia demurred immediately.

"It is all right, Papa. Thalia just had a little accident, but she is fine," Rose said, trying to push her youngest sister toward the stairs before her father could see the state of her dress and hair. But it was too late for that too.

"Rose! Whose coat is that you are wearing? And Thalia! My girl, what happened? Reynolds! Hot water, quick."

"Oh yes, Reynolds, Thalia is going to need a bath right away." Rose said, ignoring her father's questions.

"On my way, Miss Grace," the butler said, slipping past them all on his way to the kitchen.

Lord Pemberton–Howe moved to get a closer look at his youngest daughter. Immediately, his hand went up to his nose. "Oh, my dear, the stench! And you are soaking wet."

"I, er, fell into the river. But I am perfectly fine. I swim quite well, only..."

"Only?"

Thalia looked down at the puddle she was making on the floor. "Only my dress got caught on something and a gentleman had to jump in to save me."

"He was so brave, Papa, and handsome," Laia gushed. "*Especially* soaking wet."

"What? Who was this gentleman? Did you get his name?"

"It is perfectly all right, Papa. It was Mr. Fotheringay–Phipps, whom we met the other night," Rose said, giving Laia a quelling look. "Now, please, Papa, Thalia should not stand here any longer. We must get her out of those clothes and into a hot bath."

"Oh, yes, yes, of course." Her father backed away, allowing the girls to pass by him in the narrow hall.

Before they could get to the top of the stairs, however, he called up, "Rose, I would like to see you in the library as soon as may be."

"Yes, sir," Rose answered with a sigh, before following Laia to the room she shared with Thalia.

She had hoped her father wouldn't find out about this particular little adventure. It was difficult enough taking care of her younger sisters, but to have to explain everything to her father as well...

If only he didn't worry so, she thought. But years of experience of dealing with Rose and her sisters had taught him well; they may be just girls, but they did rather have a penchant for getting into trouble.

Rose quickly saw Thalia into the bath and then left her to the care of Laia and their only maid.

Entering her own room, Rose felt like doing nothing more than collapsing into her own bed. But she was still wet, from having clasped her sister to her after she had been pulled from the river, and her father was waiting for her downstairs.

She slowly pulled off Fungy's coat, but she could not resist the temptation to press the warm wool to her nose. It smelled like him, musky and clean. It was a lovely smell, although just now it was tinged a bit with the smell of that awful dirty river. She carefully folded the coat, to be returned later, and set it aside.

Quickly divesting herself of her own dirty muslin dress and underclothes, she bathed herself, using the mug of warm water she had taken from her sister's clean bath.

It was turning out to be much more difficult to watch out for her sisters here in London than she had anticipated. She had always known that her mother had, at times, wanted to tear her hair out at the girls' tomfoolery. But she had never realized how much worrying was a part of caring for someone.

She loved her sisters dearly, and she would continue to do her best in spite of their efforts to get into trouble. But really, it was past time that they learned to behave like proper young ladies.

The thought made Rose stop. It was not too long ago that she would have thought this the greatest lark, if not for the fact that Fungy and Thalia had nearly drowned. But somehow, now that she was the one responsible, it no longer seemed so much like fun. Now she saw how inappropriate such behavior was—and why. If she and her sisters were to marry well, they could not afford for society to see them behaving this way. It was not acceptable.

Just the thought of that sent a chill through Rose. Her mother had never strongly reprimanded Rose or insisted that she behave herself when she was Thalia's age, and Rose had, naturally, never minded. But now, she knew she was seriously lacking in her social education. She would have to see that her sisters did not have the same problems as she did when they became old enough to make their debuts into society.

Rose stopped in the middle of lacing her corset. In less than two years, Laia would be old enough to make her come-out. Already she had more than a healthy interest in men. Rose didn't just need to marry a man who was wealthy, but preferably one who had a mother or older sister who could help Rose oversee the girls' social education and entrance into society.

Rose resumed tying her corset. She was just pulling a clean dress over her head when there was a little knock and Laia crept into the room.

"Rose? I just wanted to apologize for my behavior earlier," she said quietly.

Rose turned and gave her sister a hug. "It is all right, Laia. Here, help me with my buttons."

She turned her back to her sister, so that she could button up the back of her dress.

"Life was so much easier when we had more maids," Laia said, trying to change the subject.

Rose would not allow it. "Laia, I know it is difficult to behave properly sometimes. But really, you must try to restrain yourself. You are old enough now to know better."

Rose sat down in the chair at her dressing table and began pulling the pins from her hair.

Laia stood behind her and picked up Rose's hairbrush. "I know. It's just that sometimes I forget. And the officers on that ship looked so handsome in their uniforms..."

Rose gave her a little smile in the mirror. It was enjoyable watching handsome men dressed in uniforms. She could not deny it. Sometimes even she indulged as well. She closed her eyes, allowing herself to relax and enjoy the feeling of her long hair being brushed. "And how typical it is of you to notice, even from that distance," she teased, unable to resist.

Laia gave a guilty giggle, lowering her gaze. "And of course, you did not notice how well Fungy looked after he climbed out of the water?"

Rose felt herself color. "Well..." She fiddled with her hairpins on the table in front of her.

"I saw the way you looked at him... And the way he looked at you, in your nearly transparent dress before you put on his coat."

"Laia!" Her own cheeks flushed bright red in the mirror.

"But he is very handsome. And he was so brave to jump into the river to save Thalia. You are lucky, Rose, to have found a husband so quickly!"

Rose looked up at her sister's reflection and swallowed hard. "What do you mean? I have not found a husband."

"But Fungy..."

"I am not going to marry him, Laia," Rose said flatly, ignoring the hollow feeling in her stomach.

"Why not? He may have been a little rude, but as you said, he was probably just tired and wanted to go home to change." Laia put the last pin into place to hold up the simple knot into which she had twisted her sister's hair.

Rose thought about Fungy, and tried to put her misgivings into words.

"It is true that he is a very kind man, and for what he did today I shall forever be in his debt, but..." Rose got up from her dressing table and walked slowly across the small room toward the door. "But he is a *dandy*. He is all posturing and airs—more concerned about how he looks, and how he is perceived by others, than about anything else. I am not at all certain that he engages his mind very often, if ever. Truly, I could not marry a man like that." Not when there was Lord Kirtland to compare him to.

"You would prefer someone more intellectual, like Papa?" Laia asked.

Rose turned back to her sister and smiled. "Yes. And besides, we don't even know what sort of fortune Fungy has, if any. Even if I decide on Fungy, or on anyone else, there is the small problem of making sure they would want to propose to me in the first place, isn't there? I must go down and face our father before he wonders what has become of me."

Eight

Rose slowly made her way down the stairs, her mind churning with thoughts of Fungy, Lord Kirtland, and her need to marry quickly. She did wonder what sort of fortune Fungy had. There was probably a way to find out.

Of course, she wouldn't need that information if she decided to marry Lord Kirtland. He, she was certain, was quite wealthy. Why, someone who could stake five hundred pounds in a card game had to have quite a fortune.

She knew she could never even dream of winning so much. However, she did hope to have the opportunity of winning at least enough to cover their bills and give her a little more time to find a husband. She just had to find a way to do so.

She wondered if she could ask her father to bring her into the card room at the next ball they went to. If not, she supposed she could ask Lord Kirtland if he knew of a way for her to play cards again.

She paused just inside her father's study. He was standing with one foot on the fender, staring into the empty fireplace, a drink in his hand. She noticed that he was wearing his old breeches, and a shabby, if serviceable, brown coat. His boots had seen better days, too—although she was sure Reynolds, who was now acting as his lordship's valet as well as their butler, had done the best he could with the old things.

No, she could not ask her father for help. He had enough troubles on his shoulders already. It would have to be Lord Kirtland to whom she would turn.

Lord Pemberton–Howe turned around with a start. "Oh, Rose! I did not hear you come in."

He gestured for her to sit down on the dark green sofa, but stayed standing by the fireplace himself.

"I want to know precisely what occurred at the docks, Rose," her father said, in his most serious manner.

"It was an accident, Papa, just as we told you. Thalia just leaned a little too far out over the water and fell in," Rose said. It was nearly true, and this way he would not worry overmuch.

Her father looked at her searchingly. It was clear that he knew there was more to the story than what she was telling him.

Finally, giving in, he set his drink down on the mantelpiece "Very well," he sighed. "I am certain you are doing your best to watch after your sisters. I know your mother was always worried about the tricks the three of you got up to. But you know your own sisters, and I trust you to look after them. It's not easy, but I know you will do the best you can."

Rose did not say a word. She could not bear to let her father know how difficult it was for her to have this responsibility. He already had enough to be anxious about; she refused to impose her own misgivings on him as well.

Looking as strained as he had the last time they had talked in the library, her father sat down on the sofa next to her. Rose felt a rush of warm affection and concern for her father. He was so brilliant despite how impractical he was, and he was trying so hard to be a good parent to her and her sisters.

Putting a comforting hand on his arm, she said, "It will be all right, Papa."

He nodded and patted her hand. "It is not so easy for a man such as I to raise three girls by myself. But I know I can count on you to help me."

He then turned to her and gave her a sly smile. "Now tell me about Fungy."

Rose just shook her head and laughed.

Fungy surfaced from the deepest sleep, coming to consciousness as slowly as he had swum up from under the surface of the river.

He sat up with a start and took in a deep breath of air.

It was all right. He was in his own bed. The binds around his legs were only his covers, not the rope that had held him under the water. Quickly, he pulled his legs free, throwing back the blankets and reveling in the feel of the cool air.

The murky light of the waning day seeped in through the mostly closed drapes. Fungy's stomach rumbled with hunger.

Donning his dressing gown, he found his valet, Thomas, in the small kitchen attempting to save his waistcoat from the rubbish heap.

Fungy always felt like Gulliver in the land of the Lilliputians whenever he walked into the little kitchen that was Thomas's kingdom. Everything was small, even the dapper valet, who stood a full foot shorter than him.

Thomas looked up as he entered the room. "It may be hopeless, sir," he informed Fungy. "Even if I got all the dirt off, the stench would be sure to linger. And the embroidery is so delicate that I would be afraid it would be quite ruined were I to attempt to wash it."

Fungy caressed the waistcoat like an old friend, but then handed it back to the valet. "Do not bother with it anymore, then, Thomas. Simply throw it away."

The man slouched forward for a moment in resignation, but he quickly regained his erect posture, and sighed, "Yes, sir."

He folded the destroyed garment and put it out of sight.

"I am famished. Is there anything to eat?"

"Certainly, sir. If you would wait for just a few moments in the drawing room, I will bring out a cold collation of meat and cheese."

Fungy nodded and went back out to the drawing room—where everything was once again of a normal size. He sat down in his favorite chair by the fire, next to which stood a table littered with the day's newspapers, all opened to the gossip pages. There were also a couple of books, lying face down to the pages where he had stopped reading. He had searched through his old trunks a few days earlier, and found a gold mine of all his old favorite books.

Idly, he picked up Socrates' rendering of Plato's *Apology*. But deciphering the original Greek was too much of an effort just now. He was sure it would come easily to him once again, but he needed a bit more practice.

Tossing it back onto the table, he reached for a newspaper, and turned it back to the front to read what was happening in the world around him.

Thomas came in with his food, and Fungy ate and read in silence—until the unbidden thoughts that had haunted him while under the murky depths of the Thames slid into his consciousness once more.

No legacy. No wife or children. No occupation. What have I done with my life? Who will remember me when I'm gone?

The words echoed over and over in his mind. In desperation, Fungy jumped from his chair, striding to the window. There must be some way to shut out these nagging voices. He leaned his fevered head against the cool glass of the window, and closed his eyes.

And there she was. Rose Grace. Her face hovered behind his eyelids, looking so worried and fearful as she called out his name, begging him to return to the dock.

She really was quite lovely. It had been absolutely impossible to look up into that face and then consign himself to the depths of the river.

Fungy opened his eyes and looked out into the street. People walked by, carriages carrying ladies home from their shopping expeditions drove past—an ordinary day for most, and yet such an extraordinary one for him.

A knock on the door jarred Fungy out of his pensive mood. He waited and heard another man's voice in the hall. Julian, Lord Huntley, entered the room, looking ready for the evening in his dark blue coat with a pair of matching pantaloons.

"Hello, Fungy. I hope you don't mind me dropping by—I just wanted to see how you were doing."

Fungy took his friend's brown outstretched hand and held it in a firm grip for perhaps a moment longer than usual.

"You are all right, aren't you?" Julian asked, now with a worried tone to his voice.

"I shall come about, I suppose." Fungy turned around and noticed the rest of his meal still spread out on the table. "Care for something to eat?" he offered.

A Dandy In Disguise

"No, thank you. I'm off to Whites for dinner in a bit. How is it that you're not dressed? Are you sure you are all right?"

"What?" Fungy looked down at the maroon brocade dressing gown he was still wearing. He hadn't even bothered to put any slippers on his feet, preferring the feel of the solid wood floor beneath his toes after the dreadful memory of his dip in the water that morning.

"Er, yes! Quite all right. Come along then, and keep me company while I dress."

Julian followed him to his bedchamber, and then settled down on a chair while Fungy pulled clothes out of his drawers and wardrobe at random.

Julian sat up, watching him closely. Fungy noticed that his blue eyes were now full of concern, and wondered how much he could unburden himself.

"What happened this morning, Fungy? What is wrong?"

Fungy randomly tossed a dark green coat on top of the pale blue pantaloons on his bed, and then sat down heavily on top of them, heedless of the creases it would cause.

"I have realized that you and Sin were right, Julian," he said. "I need to do something. To marry, have children... perhaps Sin's idea of an occupation was the right one. *O de anexetastoz bioz ou biotoz anthropo*, you know."

"I'm sorry, Fungy, what was that you said?"

Fungy gave a little laugh, and translated. "*The unexamined life is not worth living.* Sorry, old man, I'm reverting to old habits. It's Greek."

Julian laughed in turn. "I see. They didn't teach us Greek in Calcutta. If you need an appropriate quotation in Bengali, though ..."

Abruptly, Fungy held up his hand to stop his friend from speaking. There was something nagging at his mind.

In a snap, he had it. He jumped up and opened the door, calling for his valet.

The man came at a run. "Yes, sir?"

"Thomas, there was a card from a Lord Halsbury in the pocket of my waistcoat, the one I wore to Lady Anson's soiree..." Fungy began.

The man nodded and immediately went to his shaving table and pulled a card from one corner of the mirror. "You mean this one, sir?"

Fungy took it. "Yes. Indeed, this is the one. Thank you, Thomas."

The man nodded and then went to straighten the clothes Fungy had tossed onto his bed. He shook out the blue pantaloons and then offered them to his employer to put on.

"So, you are going to start looking about for a wife?" Julian asked, hesitantly.

Fungy stopped to button his pantaloons, thoughts furiously swirling around in his mind, visions of Georgiana, his first love. No one had ever been able to compare to her beauty in Fungy's eyes. No one had ever been as intelligent, sweet, *and* thoughtful . In fifteen years he had not been attracted to another woman. For fifteen years he had remained faithful to his first love. Was he really willing to give up his steadfast devotion?

Not willing, perhaps, he decided, but it was something he would have to do.

"Yes, I actually did meet a fascinating young woman, Miss Rose Grace." The name just slipped out of his mouth.

"I don't believe I know her," Julian said.

A Dandy In Disguise

"Extremely intelligent. Father is the famous archeologist Lord Pemberton–Howe. Just back from Greece." Fungy knew he was justifying her existence in his mind to himself as much as he was to Julian. But really, he thought, it was natural that she would be the first young lady he thought of, he had, after all, seen her only that morning.

"I've never thought of you as fancying the blue–stocking sort."

Fungy gave a shrug. "There is also Miss Halsbury—you know, the Parliamentarian's daughter. Very sweet girl," Fungy said, forcing himself to go through *all* of the young ladies he'd met recently.

"I've met her. Rather quiet, isn't she?"

Fungy reached for the neckcloth Thomas was offering him.

"Yes," he said, as he tied a simple knot in the starched linen. He tried to think of other young ladies, but his mind kept going back to Miss Grace.

He paused for a moment before slipping his arms into the waistcoat Thomas was holding out for him. The man was about to return the green coat to the wardrobe, but Fungy absently took it from him, while trying to remove the vision of Miss Grace in her soaking wet dress from his mind. Somehow it refused to budge.

As the valet began to protest, Fungy continued, "Can't think of anyone else who has caught my eye recently. Imagine there will be more if I look about."

"Yes." Julian tilted his head to one side. "Er, Fungy, that coat with those pantaloons...?"

Fungy having just slipped his arms into the coat, took a look in his mirror. He frowned at his reflection.

"Won't do at all, will it?" he said, with a little laugh.

Julian burst out laughing as well. "You are a cad! You nearly had me going there!"

Fungy gave his friend a rueful smile. He shook off the coat and gave it apologetically back to Thomas.

He really needed to watch himself if he both wanted to attract a young lady and keep his friends from worrying overmuch. Luckily, Julian had just thought that he was funning.

But, in fact, he had not been watching, or caring about what he was doing. It was very unlike him — or rather, very like he had once been. But again, it was not every day that one nearly died and had to completely reprioritize one's life.

Nine

"How kind of you to call, my lord," Rose said as she sat back down on the dark red–and–white striped sofa of the drawing room. Lord Kirtland took the seat opposite her in the matching chair.

Clasping her hands together tightly in her lap, Rose tried to calm herself. She desperately wished that Laia was next to her to support her in what she had to do, but she was across the room, with Aunt Farmington hovering over her, gaily entertaining the two other gentleman callers. And besides, Rose had not yet told her sisters about either Lord Kirtland or her gambling.

But at least he had finally come! She had been so afraid he wouldn't visit, especially after quite a few of the other gentlemen she'd met the other night had already come and left that afternoon. Lord Kirtland was the only one she truly wanted to see, so naturally he had been the very last one to call.

Rose had had a difficult time sitting still and being polite to all of the people who had visited during their *at–home*. All afternoon, she'd jumped up each time another guest arrived, but now, finally, Lord Kirtland was here.

Rose took a deep breath. Now, for the next step. How could she bring card–playing into the discussion, and dare she introduce it into the general conversation?

No, she quickly decided. If she was going to find out where to play cards, she had to speak to Lord Kirtland privately. She remembered what her father had said—that it was inappropriate for young ladies to want to play cards and gamble.

But it was essential that she arrange something this afternoon, she simply wouldn't get another chance, and those bills were weighing on her mind.

"I was disappointed to find you not at home yesterday, Miss Grace," Lord Kirtland was saying, as Rose handed him a cup of tea.

He was looking as handsome as ever, neatly and fashionably dressed, still causing her little shivers every time he looked at her with those dark eyes. "Oh, my sisters and I had gone to see about our household goods, my lord. They are being shipped from Greece. Unfortunately, the ship has not yet arrived."

Rose forced a smile onto her face, trying to hide her anxiety. This was definitely going to be difficult. Bound by convention, she was forced to sit and make polite conversation, but it was unquestionably the most arduous exchange she had ever had.

Luckily, Rose and Lord Kirtland were sitting quite by themselves. She wondered if she dared to quickly change the subject while she had the opportunity.

Before she could continue however, Lord Kirtland replied easily, "I am sorry to hear that. I hope that it arrives soon. May I ask if you have brought back any interesting artifacts from your father's expeditions?" he asked. He was sitting back comfortably with his tea, completely unaware of her tension.

"Oh, no. The most significant objects were immediately handed over to the government. Unlike Lord Elgin, my father does not believe in stealing precious artifacts from Greece."

"Old Lord Elgin *stole* the marbles?" Lord Strapton asked dimly, arranging his lanky limbs in the spindly chair next to Lord Kirtland. He was followed by Laia, happily leaning on the arm of young Lieutenant Wroughtly, with her aunt quietly bringing up the rear.

Rose groaned silently. She had lost her opportunity.

But Lord Kirtland had also seized upon Rose's statement. His voice rising slightly, he proclaimed, "Lord Elgin did *not* steal the marble relics from Greece, Miss Grace. He rescued them."

Rose's nails bit into her palms, temper flaring at his tone. This was a very touchy subject among archeologists, but it was one that she and felt strongly about, and that she was absolutely confident in.

She kept her tone deliberately moderate and polite. "That is what he claims, my lord. However, there are others in the archaeological society who feel..."

"Oh, in the archaeological society!" Lord Strapton said, with a dismissive air—not, Rose thought, that he knew anything about the society at all. "Well, of course, *they* would hold odd views about the subject."

Lord Kirtland frowned at the gentleman. Clearly, he too knew that Strapton was totally ignorant about the subject. "There are differing viewpoints even within the archaeological society, Strapton. And I believe that Lord Elgin should be commended for saving the marbles from falling further into ruin and be rewarded handsomely for doing so."

Laia gasped, but Rose immediately put a hand on her sister's knee while simultaneously biting back her own sharp retort. While she would have dearly liked to have engaged Lord Kirtland in an argument on the topic, this was not the time—she needed him too badly just now to alienate him in any way.

"Miss Grace, do you plan on attending Lady Yarborough's soiree tomorrow night?" Lieutenant Wroughtly asked.

Rose threw him a grateful look. He had — rather wisely — stayed out of the argument, and for once his polite, meaningless conversation was exactly what was needed. She was only worried about how besotted Laia looked as she gazed at him.

"I had rather hoped that you would attend Mrs. Cartwright's rout, don't you know, so that I might have another opportunity to dance with you," Lord Strapton added, giving Rose his usual, vacuously charming, smile.

"I am deeply flattered, gentlemen, truly I am. But my aunt and I have not yet decided which party we shall be attending tomorrow. Have we, Aunt Farmington?"

"No, my dear, but I was thinking that we should try to pay our respects to both hostesses."

"Oh, but Mrs. Cartwright's routs are really quite out of the ordinary," Lord Strapton said with conviction.

"Not any more so than Lady Yarborough's soirees," the Lieutenant argued.

This was the opportunity Rose had been waiting for.

While the two men carried on their good–natured argument, with Laia and Aunt Farmington proffering their opinions, Rose turned back to Lord Kirtland and said quietly, so that only he could hear her, "My lord, I was actually hoping that you would know of some place where I might go to play cards once again. I have to admit, I truly enjoyed myself the other evening."

He leaned forward so that they might have a more private conversation. Unfortunately, his discreet words were not what Rose wanted to hear.

"I am happy you enjoyed our little game, Miss Grace. However, it is not strictly proper for a you to play cards."

He reached forward and helped himself to a slice of cake. "In fact, I was quite surprised that your father brought you into the card room at Lady Bascombe's ball. It is quite unheard of for a young lady to play cards at a ball; dancing is a far more likely, and more appropriate pursuit."

"Oh, well, I did dance quite a bit that evening, but I had grown tired. My father was kind enough to offer to escort me into the card room for a rest," Rose said, fudging a little on the details. She was not sure how Lord Kirtland would react if she told him that her father had only brought her into the card room on a lark—he might very well be one of those straight-laced gentleman who stuck to the rules.

Kirtland gave a nod, his mouth too full of cake to comment.

"But is a ball the only place I could play?" Rose persisted.

Kirtland took a sip of tea. "No, there are card parties. I am actually attending one on Tuesday evening, hosted by Lady Kemble. But again, I do not believe that it is at all proper for a young lady such as yourself to attend."

Lord Strapton interrupted their quiet conversation by coughing obviously. The gentlemen's argument had clearly been resolved, and he was ready to leave. As he stood up and made his parting comments, Rose stood as well and walked him to the door of the room. "Thank you so much for coming, my lord."

"Thank you, Miss Grace. May I be assured of a dance tomorrow evening at the rout?"

"Yes, of course, if we decide to attend that party, I shall be very happy to meet you there," Rose said easily. Even if he was not the most interesting man she had ever met, and held rather odd ideas about archaeology, at least she would not be a wallflower the entire evening.

"Oh, and though it may not be strictly proper, there is going to be a masquerade at Vauxhall Gardens next week..."

"Absolutely not!" her aunt said firmly from behind her.

Rose gave a little giggle and a shrug. "It was a good try, my lord." It was such a shame that Aunt Farmington knew her so well. There surely could be nothing more fun than a masquerade.

The young man looked a little taken aback by her aunt's forcefulness and left quickly. As she closed the door behind him, an idea started tickling in the back of Rose's mind.

She went back to Lord Kirtland, who was finishing off his cake. They still had some privacy, since Laia was flirting with the dashing young officer, and Aunt Farmington had returned to her side in order to keep a sharp eye on the proceedings.

"My lord," she said quietly, refilling his cup of tea, "what if I attended the card party in a mask and domino? That way no one would know who I was."

Lord Kirtland thought about this for a moment, nodding his head. "I have known ladies to do so in order to maintain their anonymity. Of course, you would need a gentleman to vouch for you..."

Rose batted her eyelashes at Lord Kirtland, and began to try to think of other ways she might convince him to take her, if that didn't work.

None were necessary, thankfully. Although he looked dubious for a moment, he relented at her sweet, pleading smile.

"Very well, Miss Grace, if that is what you truly wish to do?"

"Oh, yes!" she said quickly.

"I am not at all sure..."

"Please, my lord?"

He stole a look at her aunt.

"I assure you, no one need know," Rose said.

He nodded. "Then I shall be honored to take you—if you wear a mask and domino."

"Oh, thank you, so very much, my lord. I truly do appreciate it."

His answering smile was all she needed.

Rose had a hard time not bouncing in her seat, she was so excited. Everything was working out exactly the way she had hoped.

Ten

After Lord Kirtland and Lieutenant Wroughtly had left, Rose went to her room to try to rest in preparation for her outing to the opera that evening, but her mind was whirling with thoughts of Lord Kirtland and the impending card party.

"What was it that you and Lord Kirtland were whispering about?" Laia demanded barging into her room, followed, inevitably, by Thalia. Her sisters could always be counted on to insist on being included in everything. Thalia looked expectantly at her as well.

"Oh, we were discussing something that occurred at Lady Bascombe's ball the other night," Rose said, as innocently as she could. But, as she expected, it was not enough for her overly curious little sisters, who folded their arms and looked pointedly at her in unison. Rose nearly laughed, but managed to stifle it. And she did have to admit she wanted to share her excitement with them as much as they clearly wanted to hear it.

"Well," Rose began, "after I had danced for some time at the ball the other night, Aunt Farmington found an old friend of hers and fobbed me off onto Papa. I told him that I was bored with dancing, so he was kind enough to bring me into the card room with him. It was there that I met Lord Kirtland and a friend of his, Mr. Aiken. They taught me how to play whist and…"

She paused for effect, and then, smiling at their rapt faces, continued, "...and I managed to win nearly thirty pounds!"

Thalia gasped, while Laia's pale green eyes began to sparkle with excitement. "You won? I can't believe..."

"Why can't you? Rose is extremely intelligent. Why shouldn't she win at cards?" Thalia said, suddenly very defensive.

"There is no reason why she shouldn't. I'm just surprised she did," Laia said. "So that's what the two of you were talking about?" she asked Rose.

Rose nodded. "Yes. I asked him if he knew of some place where I might gamble again. I told him I enjoyed playing cards so much the other night that I was looking for another opportunity to do so. He was very kind, and offered to take me to a card party on Tuesday evening, so long as I wear a mask."

"Wait, I'm confused," Thalia said, bouncing on the bed. "Why do you want to play cards with Lord Kirtland? I thought you were interested in Fungy!"

Rose frowned at Laia. Clearly, she had been filling Thalia's head with romantic nonsense about her and Fungy. "No, Thalia. Lord Kirtland is wealthy and an archeologist. He is much closer to the sort of gentleman I want to marry than Fungy. And besides, I did not ask Lord Kirtland to take me to this party just to be with him. I'm hoping, if luck is with me, to win enough money to pay off our most pressing bills. And maybe even more. Maybe enough that I won't have to worry about marrying so quickly."

Understanding dawned on Thalia, and she clapped her hands in excitement. "You will win all the money we need!"

"Oh yes, Rose, do win lots of money!" Laia gushed. "Then I can go out and buy more ribbons, and Thalia can get a new hat to replace the one she lost in the river, and..."

"Laia, please! I've got to win the money first before you spend it all, *and* we've got to pay off our other bills before we mount up any new ones."

"But you will win, Rose, won't you?" Thalia asked, bouncing up and down again.

"I will certainly do my best," she said, leaning back against the pillows on her bed, fighting to control her enthusiasm while her sisters didn't even try.

Fungy began to have misgivings about coming to see Lord Halsbury as soon as his lordship started extolling Fungy's admirable qualities.

"You are a very impressive young man, from what I hear of you. Generous—dancing with the wallflowers, offering fashion advice to those who need it, and apparently, you do all this in such a way as to make everyone not feel the least awkward."

Lord Halsbury offered Fungy a glass of brandy before going on.

"Brummell, y'know, will cut a man down with just the lift of one eyebrow, and let him and all those around know that whatever he is wearing is not good enough. You, on the other hand, simply whisper a word or two into the man's ear without making a scene of it or embarrassing the poor fellow to death. And the advice always takes, because they know you mean well, and are not just a high–and–mighty arbiter of fashion. Again, very impressive," Halsbury said, hooking his thumb into the watch pocket of his dull brown waistcoat.

Fungy took a large sip of his drink. This was becoming rather embarrassing.

"And, Fotheringay–Phipps—may I call you Fungy? And there's the way you treat the young ladies. Always a kind word. Again if there is the slightest criticism, it is said in such a kind way that no one could possibly take offense. Why, you must be friends with absolutely everybody!"

"My lord, excuse me for being blunt," Fungy paused, hoping Lord Halsbury wouldn't be offended, "but you don't know me. How do you know that I've done any of these things? Don't remember seeing you at many parties."

Lord Halsbury stopped and gave Fungy a wicked smile. "I have my ways."

"Oh?" Now he was really beginning to get worried. What sort of man *was* Lord Halsbury, to have... 'ways'?

He didn't even know Halsbury, Fungy realized. All he knew was that the man was involved in politics, an active member of the House of Lords, and dressed with all the fashion sense of a country squire who rarely came to town. At least his coats were made to fit his stout figure well.

Lord Halsbury got up and pulled the bell cord that was hanging next to the fireplace. A moment later a footman walked into the room.

"James, ask my daughter to step in a moment, would you?"

The footman bowed and left on his errand.

"I believe you met Harriet at Lady Anson's, did you not?"

"Yes. She spoke with Miss Grace for some time, I believe."

"Yes, that's right. Miss Grace—now there's an interesting girl, aside from the small fact that she has a lot to learn about how to go on in society."

Fungy gave a polite little laugh, but the picture in his head of Miss Grace was that of an angel calling to him from over the edge of the river. Fungy firmly pushed that image aside and stood as Miss Halsbury came into the room. She was a quiet girl, not one to put herself forward. Of course, she did not have the looks to compete with the prettier girls in society, but she was sweet and gentle. Nothing compared to Miss Grace, of course, but few could.

"Yes, Papa, you wished to see me?" she said, as she closed the door silently behind her.

"Yes, my dear. You remember Mr. Fotheringay–Phipps, er, Fungy?"

"Of course. It is wonderful to see you again, sir." She gave him a small curtsy.

He nodded his head. "The pleasure is mine."

"Fungy wanted to know where I got my information about him and his behavior, my dear."

Miss Halsbury nodded, and gave him a shy little smile. "It is all my fault, I'm afraid."

"There you have it, Fungy. I present to you my social spy. Harriet and her mother go to all of the most fashionable parties so I don't have to. She comes back and tells me about everything and everyone she saw. She seemed to be most impressed with you on the few occasions you've met."

Miss Halsbury's cheeks turned bright pink.

"I had no idea I was being watched," Fungy admitted, rather stunned by this news. It had happened before that a young lady had shown him marked attention, but he'd easily discerned her intentions and gently redirected them to another more likely candidate. He had not realized that Miss Halsbury...

"I assure you, sir, if it were not for my father, I would not have been so bold," Miss Halsbury said quietly.

"No, no, it was not Harriet's idea to watch you in particular, Fungy. I simply asked her to look out for someone who moved among society easily, and who she thought was intelligent enough to undertake an assignment for me should the need arise."

"And you singled me out, Miss Halsbury?" Fungy was becoming more surprised by the moment.

"Of course, Fungy," Miss Halsbury said, looking as if it was obvious that he was the right man for such work.

"How could you possibly think that I was so intelligent?" he could not help asking.

Miss Halsbury's already–pink cheeks turned even brighter, but her voice was quite serious when she said, "You try to hide behind your façade of ennui, but I can see your intelligence in your eyes and in the clever things that you say. You are also very careful in the way you treat people—always thoughtful, so as not to hurt anyone's feelings or embarrass them publicly."

"As you see, Fungy, my daughter is an excellent judge of character. I trust her implicitly," Lord Halsbury concurred.

Fungy was stunned. Just from watching him, Miss Halsbury had discerned all this, and clearly thought him capable and responsible enough to take on whatever assignment her father might need him for.

And yet his own cousin did not trust him.

Merry had bypassed him in favor of Sin when it came time to choose a godfather for his son. He had thought Fungy too irresponsible and incapable of taking the position seriously. He had even forgotten

Fungy's reputation for being one of the brightest students to ever attend Eton.

How had this girl seen these abilities in him, when his own cousin and best friend could not? And how could she see this just by watching him at parties? The thought astounded him.

He had also never felt so exposed in all of his life. He might as well be standing naked in front of this girl. She could see right through him!

Fungy swallowed his discomfort and turned back to his host. "What sort of, er, assignment is it that you have in mind for me, sir?"

Lord Halsbury nodded to his daughter. "Thank you, Harriet, that will be all."

Lord Halsbury got up as the door shut behind her and plucked a piece of paper off of his desk. Wordlessly, he handed it to Fungy to read. It was addressed to no one, and seemed to be more of an odd list than a letter.

On it were written the names of a number of lesser–known young men, usually younger sons or brothers of wealthy peers, and some older ladies who were not prominent members of society but had such excellent connections that they were welcomed everywhere. Next to each name was an amount of money, anything between five hundred and five thousand pounds.

Three of the names were crossed off with a careful line running through their names. At the top it said, "To watch" and at the bottom were the initials *PH*.

Fungy looked it over twice before turning his gaze in askance at Lord Halsbury.

"It is a list of targets—or victims, if you will—of a gambling scheme that I believe is being very cleverly run from within the *ton.*"

Fungy sat up.

"The names crossed off are of people who have recently disappeared from town. Disappeared, I believe, because of their financial straits."

Fungy looked at the note once more, reconsidering the crossed–off names. "The Honorable Curtis Flinchley. Yes, I've heard that he had been sent down to rusticate for a while at his father's estate. Lady Amelia Cotsworth." He thought for a minute. "I remember meeting her not two weeks ago at Lady Sefton's ball."

"Lost two thousand pounds that night and hasn't been seen since," Lord Halsbury supplied.

"My God!"

"Yes, precisely. This is nasty business, Fungy, and we don't know who is masterminding it. I am determined to find out. As yet, there are no laws against winning another's fortune at a game of cards, but some of us in Parliament are working on that as well."

"Do you know to whom she lost this money?" Fungy asked.

"No. If we knew that, it would be easy, wouldn't it? Unfortunately, she lost the money over a long night of play and, it seems, to a number of people. It is quite likely that her vowels are all being bought up by one person, or perhaps all of the people she lost to are involved in the scheme as well. It is difficult to find out for certain—which is where you come in."

"What is it you need me to do?"

"I want you to find out who is running this scheme and stop it."

Fungy nearly laughed. "You make it sound so easy."

"Oh no, Fungy, it is not easy at all. The only clue we have is his, or her, initials. But you know everyone who is anyone in the beau monde. If anyone can figure this out, I believe it is you."

Fungy sat back in his chair, taken aback by the level of trust Lord Halsbury had in him. Could he possibly do this?

Then he remembered the quiet confidence Miss Halsbury had shown in him.

He *could* do this. He was intelligent and responsible. He had vowed not a day ago to change his life to one that was more meaningful, and here was the perfect opportunity to do so.

He stood up. "I shall do it."

Lord Halsbury stood as well, and grasped Fungy's hand. "Excellent! I knew I could count on you."

Lord Kirtland smiled at Rose, but somehow it didn't make her feel any better. If anything, it made her feel worse. How could she be losing so badly and he still be smiling at her?

It was a smile of encouragement, she told herself. *Why else would he smile at me like that when I'm losing?*

She was sure that her luck would turn any moment now. It had to. She had won so many of the tricks earlier in the evening—this was just a run of bad luck. It would end very soon, it had to.

Rose took a deep breath, played a card from her hand and then returned Lord Kirtland's smile from behind her mask. She would not give up hope.

There was no reason to give up yet—aside from the fact that she had already run out of money. Lord Kirtland had already been kind enough to write a vowel on her behalf with the understanding that she would pay him back as soon as she could. And since it was to his good friend, Mr. Aiken, she was sure it would not be a problem. Certainly, by the end of the night, she would have won that money back and more. Much more.

She paused to watch Lord Kirtland play the two of spades. With it, he won the trick.

Rose had to win at least two hundred pounds in order to pay off all of her family's bills. That shouldn't be too difficult, considering the amounts being wagered. Why, she had already won and lost at least that much. Winning all that she needed was not going to be a problem.

The suit being played was diamonds. Rose didn't have any diamonds. With a little smile, she played a low trump card.

As soon as she had won her two hundred pounds, she would definitely stop, she told herself firmly. She would stop gambling—in fact, she would stop playing cards altogether. All she needed was enough to pay the bills.

Rose swallowed hard as Lord Kirtland took the trick once more, beating her trump card with one of his own. He looked so very pleased with himself, she thought with a bitterness that shamed her with its fierceness.

This was just a game to him, but she had to win this money!

Rose took a deep breath to calm herself, and looked over at Lord Kirtland once more. He was now smiling down at his cards. Well, she was glad he was pleased with his hand. She wished she was as pleased with her own.

When he looked up again, he caught her looking at him. Somehow, imperceptibly, his smile changed. His eyes narrowed a bit, a strange light coming into them, and one side of his mouth twitched higher than the other. Was it desire that she saw in his eyes? A tremor rushed through her body.

Rose quickly looked back at her cards. Randomly, she put down a card, and then immediately realized that she had made a stupid move. She had played her queen when the king hadn't been played yet.

Was she falling in love with Lord Kirtland? He certainly made her feel... there wasn't a word for it. Unsettled? No, not quite. Excited, perhaps—just a look from him could send chills up and down her spine. She had heard that people quite often feel unusual or off-balance when they fell in love. Perhaps that was what was happening to her.

Mr. Aiken played the king, winning the trick and the rubber. *Oh, dear!*

The cards were gathered, points tallied, and a new hand dealt.

Rose took a deep breath and forced herself to concentrate. She could not afford to make mistakes.

Eleven

"When your demeanor mimics the name of the game, perhaps it is time to take a break," a gentleman said, as he approached her table.

Rose had just picked up her new hand and taken a first peek at the cards she had been dealt.

She turned toward the gentleman. "Fungy!" All of her muscles, which she hadn't even realized were tense, relaxed.

He looked like a breath of fresh air, all in blue and frothy white. And just like that, her breathing eased. She couldn't help but give him a broad smile. "If you mean to imply that I was looking wistfully at my cards, then, I am afraid, I must admit my guilt."

"Then perhaps it would be best if you sat out this hand and took a stroll about with me?"

He held out his hand for her to take and she grasped onto it as if it were a lifeline. She wondered briefly if he was now saving *her* from drowning, just as he had saved Thalia a few days before.

"That sounds lovely. I am getting a bit of a headache. Some exercise would no doubt do me good."

She turned back to the others at the table, "I do hope you will excuse me…"

"Egerton! Rolly Egerton, how are you? Haven't seen you since…" a large, red–faced, jovial man interrupted Rose as he strode over to Lord Kirtland.

"Applethwaite!" Lord Kirtland exclaimed, standing up to shake his friend's hand. "Good to see you. Er, it's Kirtland, now. M'father died last year."

"Eh? Oh, sorry about that. So now you've joined high society?"

As the two went into reminiscing, Rose gave a little shrug. "I suppose now *is* a good time for a break." She placed her hand on Fungy's arm and they walked slowly toward the terrace.

"I am sorry to have interrupted your game, Miss Grace," Fungy said, as he led the way through the room.

"Oh, it is not a problem at all. As you said, I needed a break."

He nodded. "Looked as if you were having a spot of trouble."

She paused and smiled gratefully up at him. "Always there when I need you, Fungy?"

He turned his eyes on her. The look in them made her feel like someone had just enveloped her in a warm, soft blanket.

"At your service," he said, his voice as soothing as his warm blue eyes.

Rose had trouble tearing her eyes away from his. She could happily drown in those eyes.

As they stepped out onto the terrace, she stopped and took a deep breath of the warm night air. It was filled with sweet scents from the garden, and was more refreshing than anything could have been just then.

With one swift movement, she pushed back her mask from her face and the hood from her head. It felt very good to be free of the physical restrictions.

Fungy was watching her with a little smile playing on his lips.

A Dandy In Disguise

"How did you know it was me behind the mask?" she asked.

He touched the Macedonian bracelet on her arm. "This gave you away."

"Oh, yes, you admired it at Lady Anson's ball. I'd forgotten about that."

His hand lingered on her arm for a moment, sending heat rushing from that point through her body.

She felt herself leaning into him, and took a small step away instead, turning toward the garden. "I must say, it has been quite wonderful being masked. I have been able to do things that a proper young lady would never do."

"Oh? What have you been up to, Miss Grace? Not getting into any more trouble, I hope?" he asked, laughter in his voice.

Rose giggled. "Oh, no! And how could I, when no one knew it was me? No, but I walked here with only Lord Kirtland's escort. And, I hope you will not think me fast, but I have been drinking brandy!"

Fungy raised his eyebrows. "It is uncommon for a young lady to have a taste for brandy."

"I know. My father invited me to drink it with him one evening a few years ago when my mother would not—she thought it improper for a lady to do so. But he does not like to drink alone and there were no other English gentlemen with us on our last expedition, so I drank with him. Since then, when given the opportunity—which isn't often, I assure you—I partake of a little." Rose gave a little giggle.

As she had expected, Fungy was not horrified by this admission. Instead, he smiled. "I see. Must have been lonely when you were on an expedition with your father."

"Oh, no. We always had each other, my sisters and my mother. There were, sometimes, other archeologists as well. And we all worked quite hard—as hard as my father—cataloguing the things that he found." Rose paused. "That reminds me. I never properly thanked you the other day for saving my sister, Thalia."

Fungy brushed aside her words with a wave of his hand. "Think no more of it. Now tell me, what brings you here to this little gathering? Shouldn't you be dancing at Lady Southwick's ball instead?"

Rose gave him a guilty smile. "Perhaps I should. But when Lord Kirtland told me about this card party, I just had to come and see it for myself," she said, repeating the lie she had practiced just in case anyone asked her this question. "I do so like new experiences—and to be honest, I do not care for large society parties." Well, that, at least, was the truth, she thought to herself.

"Do not care for balls?" Fungy asked, clearly intrigued.

"I am not used to society. The few parties I've attended I have found to be deathly dull, I'm afraid."

"Ah. But it is all in the attitude, Miss Grace. If you go expecting to be entertained, or enlightened, then yes, they are, as you say, deathly dull. However, if you go with an eye for the absurd you shall be highly amused, I guarantee it."

She thought about this for a moment, and laughed. "Yes, I do believe that is a good way of thinking about it. I'm sure to enjoy myself if I look at things from that perspective. Thank you!"

"Seeing you happy and laughing is all the thanks that I need," he said, half to himself. He then gave a rather embarrassed little laugh. "Perhaps I should return you to your card game."

Reluctantly, she put her mask and hood back on. She loved the freedom that being masked afforded her, but she hated how uncomfortable and hot it was.

Fungy took her arm and began to lead her back inside. But just as they had stepped back into the drawing room, Lord Kirtland approached them.

"Ah, I was just coming to see where you were."

"And I was just about to return her to you, my lord," Fungy said.

Despite his words, he seemed reluctant to pass her hand over to Lord Kirtland, and held on to it for perhaps a moment too long.

Rose felt like she was being passed like a card from one player to the next, and she was not entirely sure she liked it. However, Lord Kirtland was her escort for the evening, and he had been kind enough to bring her here at her insistence, so she supposed she didn't have too much choice in the matter.

The fleeting expression of annoyance on Fungy's face told her that he did not exactly like having to give her up either.

"Have you had enough fresh air, or may I entice you to take a walk with me through the garden? It is a beautiful evening," Lord Kirtland said smoothly, his rich baritone gliding over her like a snake over a patch of sand.

It *was* a beautiful evening, and the twinkling lights in the garden had looked very enticing from the terrace, so she put aside her discomfort. Nodding her head in acquiescence, she turned and headed back outside with Lord Kirtland.

They strolled along in silence for a bit, Rose slowly feeling her muscles tense once again. What was it about Lord Kirtland that put her so much on edge?

He was very handsome, in a rough and rugged way. She supposed all those muscles would come in handy on an archaeological dig, if one wanted to do the actual digging oneself. And it was quite wonderful that Lord Kirtland was an archeologist, at all.

These positive qualities certainly spoke volumes for the way she was feeling—for she was sure that these odd, new sensations were caused by attraction to Lord Kirtland. How could she not be when he fit so many of the criteria she was looking for in a husband?

Yes, perhaps that was it. She was just nervous because she knew that he was the perfect man for her.

She smiled up at him as they walked slowly, enjoying the star–strewn night and the garden. Rose willed herself to relax and enjoy the evening.

How wonderful this was, the perfect man for her taking her for a romantic walk through a moonlit garden. She chided herself for feeling anything but pure happiness in the moment. *Just stop thinking, Rose, and enjoy the evening and the company.*

She was doing exactly what she should be doing. She may not be winning at cards, but she was winning a husband. With that comforting thought, she allowed herself to enjoy the garden.

The wonderful smell Rose had noticed from the terrace came from the rose bushes lining the walkway. Now, out amongst them, the smell was even more wonderful and intense. The crunching of the gravel beneath their feet was the only sound around them, lending a peaceful, calming feeling to their surroundings.

"A more perfect evening, I could not imagine," Rose said, gazing up at the sky.

A Dandy In Disguise

"Indeed," Lord Kirtland said, "I feel humbled to be among such beautiful things." He wasn't looking at the stars.

"I hope I did not ruin your game when I left the table," Rose said, deliberately changing the subject.

"No, not at all. Quite all right. My friend, Mr. Applethwaite, took your place for some time." He paused and then said, "I am sorry that I did not notice that you had become tired."

"I think I was simply concentrating too hard on the cards. I suppose I'm not used to playing for such a long time."

"No? Do you not play with your sisters?"

"Not whist. We would play casino sometimes, and other children's games. But they are just silliness and fun."

"Yes."

Rose stopped speaking. She had been meaning to make a joke of playing such games, but Lord Kirtland did not seem to be the sort one joked with. He was not at all like Fungy, who was always making light of a situation or joking. Lord Kirtland seemed to be more of a serious type of person. Perhaps staidness came with a title and wealth.

She brushed it aside and focused on enjoying their walk.

As they neared the end of the walkway, Lord Kirtland took her hand from his arm and turned to face her. If he moved even a few inches closer their bodies would be touching, Rose thought with a slight tremor, but she stood her ground and resisted the urge to step away.

"I am so very glad you were able to come with me this evening," he said quietly, putting his hands on her shoulders and pulling her even closer toward him.

Rose swallowed and wondered if he was going to kiss her. "It was very kind of you to bring me."

He bent his head forward, his lips slowly coming closer to hers.

Yes, he was going to kiss her!

His hot breath smelled of the wine he had been drinking.

Rose fought the urge to recoil. She could do this. She was attracted to this man. She wanted to marry him.

At the last moment Rose turned her head so that he kissed her cheek.

What was wrong with her? She was about to receive her first kiss from a handsome man who would make the most perfect husband and solve all of her family's problems. Why could she not kiss him?

He pulled back and chuckled. It was not a very happy sound, however.

"I am sorry, my lord, I, I think..."

"Maidenly modesty?" he said, interrupting her.

Rose exhaled with a sigh of relief and then gave a nervous little laugh. "Yes, I suppose that is it. Could—could we go back to the card game? I still owe Mr. Aiken two hundred pounds and I would like to win it back from him."

Twelve

The following morning, Rose was awoken by both of her sisters jumping onto her bed.

She moaned and turned over so that she was face down, and covered her head with her quilt.

"Come on, Rose, we have let you sleep long enough. Now you have to tell us how you did last night," Thalia said, shaking her shoulder roughly.

"Yes, and who you met," Laia urged.

"How much money did you win?"

"Did Lord Kirtland kiss you?"

"Go away!" Rose said from under her covers.

"No!" the two girls said in unison.

"Not until you tell us everything," Laia said.

"I think we should go to the park today. You have been putting us off for long enough. Surely you have met enough gentlemen now so that we may go and choose among them," Thalia said eagerly. "Come on, Rose. Do say that we might go today, please?"

"Oh yes, please Rose, we should definitely go to the park this afternoon," Laia agreed enthusiastically. "Unless there is a gentleman who has invited you out for a drive?"

Rose felt like she was suffocating, so she lowered her covers and turned over. "No, I have not been invited out by anyone." She sighed. "All right, we may go for a ride this afternoon." She paused and then added, "But you both must promise to be on your best behavior, or else I shall never take you to the park during the promenade ever again!"

"Why Rose, whatever makes you think that we would not behave properly?" Thalia asked innocently.

Both Rose and Laia gave her such a look that very soon all three girls were giggling away.

"But you still haven't told us about last night," Laia complained.

"Yes. How much money did you win?" Thalia asked again.

Rose sat up, propping her pillows behind her. She then clasped her hands in her lap and stared down at them unable to look her sisters in the eye. "I didn't win any. In fact, I lost all that I had and more, I'm afraid."

"And more? How could you lose more than you had?" Laia gasped.

"Lord Kirtland had to pay my debt to his friend, Mr. Aiken, and accepted a vowel from me—a promissory note saying that I would pay him one hundred pounds."

"One hundred—" Laia started to scream.

Rose immediately clasped her hand over her sister's mouth. "Shhh! If Aunt Farmington or Papa were to hear you…"

"Oh, Rose! Where are you going to get so much money?" Thalia asked in a whisper.

"I don't know. I suppose I'll just have to win it back. I had lost two hundred to him, but then won back half of it."

"Oh, well that is good, I suppose," Laia said, a little uncertainly.

"Was Fungy there?" Thalia asked.

"Yes, he was. He took me out for a breath of air on the terrace," Rose admitted.

Laia squeaked. "He did? How romantic!"

Rose thought about that for a moment and then said, "No, it really wasn't very romantic. It was just very pleasant. He is a very kind man, and makes me laugh."

"And makes you feel good? Does he give you tingles?" Laia asked.

"Laia! You should not know of such things!" Rose scolded her sister.

"Well, but does he?" she persisted.

Rose smiled. "He does make me feel good. But then Lord Kirtland took me for a walk through the garden and that was *very* romantic."

"Did he kiss you?" Laia asked, scrunching up closer.

"No! He is a gentleman. He would not do that unless he had asked me to marry him first," Rose lied. She was not about to admit to her sisters that she had backed out of her first kiss.

"Do you know what Lord Kirtland said when I was losing?" Rose asked her sisters, quickly trying to get away from the subject of kissing. "He laughed and said that it was just a game, as if there was no money involved."

"My goodness, he *must* have a lot of money to think so little of it," Thalia cooed.

"My thoughts exactly."

"So you think he is the one you should marry, Rose?" Laia asked.

Rose nodded. "I am thinking very seriously of it. He is as close to my ideal husband as I'm going to find at such short notice."

Her sisters sat back quietly thinking about this, as did Rose.

She was certain that this was the right answer, and if he didn't make her feel as comfortable as Fungy did, well, perhaps she would be more at ease with him after they had known each other a little longer.

The rhythmic thwacking sound of the punching bag lulled Fungy into a mindless haze. Once he had got into the rhythm, he no longer needed to think. The physical release of the constant punching was very relaxing.

Right. Left. Right. Left. Right, right. Left, left.

As his mind started to drift off among the quiet hubbub of Gentleman Jackson's Boxing Salon, Fungy noticed that this was not as relaxing as it normally was.

Perhaps it was him. He had had a most difficult time of it recently. In a very short period of time his entire life had been turned upside down.

But what still disturbed him the most was...

"Good morning, Fungy."

...Merry.

Fungy stopped hitting the punching bag just in front of his face. Turning he saw his cousin and Sin strolling past him on their way to the punching bags next to his.

"Doing well," Sin said, shedding his coat and waistcoat.

"He always has excellent form," Merry commented, taking off his own coat.

"Good morning, gentlemen," Fungy said coldly.

Merry paused to look at him before taking off his waistcoat. "Haven't seen you around recently. Is everything all right?"

"Fine. Just fine, thank you. Yourself?" Fungy asked, trying to keep his voice neutral.

"I've been well."

"Teresa and the baby?"

"They are doing very well. Teresa finally settled on a nursemaid, so we have all been getting more sleep."

"Glad to hear that." Fungy turned back to the bag, but it no longer looked so interesting.

He took a step toward his cousin. "Care to spar with me, Merry?"

Both men turned in surprise to him.

"*You* want to fight, Fungy?" Sin asked.

"Yes, is there a problem with that?"

"No, it is just that I don't believe I've ever seen you actually sparring with anyone before. You usually just work the bag."

"Today I am in the mood for something different," he shrugged. "What do you say, Cousin?"

Merry gave him a little bow. "I would be happy to." He then gave Fungy a teasing smile. "Do you really think you stand a chance? I'm a bit heavier than you are."

"No matter. I can take you on," Fungy responded quickly.

Merry laughed. "That's what you always said when we were little and I would still always beat you."

Fungy found nothing amusing in this. He just flexed his hands. "And I thought you had completely forgotten our youth."

With that parting shot, he stepped into the ring in the center of the room, and waited for his cousin to join him.

"What was that supposed to mean?" Merry asked, following him.

"Only that you and Sin both seemed to have conveniently forgotten both our youth and me." He hit Merry hard across his jaw.

Merry wasn't prepared, and he dropped to the floor like a stone.

Sin jumped into the ring to help him up. "I say, Fungy, that was not fair."

"Why not? He should have been ready." Fungy moved from foot to foot. "Come on, Merry. What's your problem? Have you forgotten your boast of just a moment ago, as well?"

Merry shrugged Sin off of him and put up his fists, now ready for an earnest fight. "I don't know what your problem is, Fungy, but if you want a fight, I'm ready."

Merry ended up mostly defending himself, as Fungy held nothing back. In a surge of flying fists, he released all of his anger and hurt on his cousin.

How could Merry think him irresponsible? Hook right. How could he not trust him? Uppercut left. Why could an utter *stranger* see through his façade while his own best friend and cousin whom he had grown up with could not see past it? He punched him a doubler with a quick left–right combination, coming down hard.

How was it that Merry had so conveniently forgotten how responsible Fungy had been when they were together in school? All he saw now was Fungy's precise dressing and his outward demeanor of ennui. Merry had forgotten who St. John Fotheringay–Phipps really was—and that hurt more than anything else.

Fungy landed another well–placed right hook to his cousin's jaw and Merry went down, but Fungy wasn't finished. He dropped to one knee and continued pummeling his cousin, giving free rein to all of his latent anger.

He was past caring or even thinking about what he was actually doing. All he cared about now was beating out all of his fury on the one who had caused it.

A strong hand grabbed his arm as he was about to land another blow to Merry's jaw, and pulled him back and to his feet.

He spun around, ready to attack whoever it was who had pulled him away, but found his nose within inches of Gentleman Jackson himself. The man, although shorter than Fungy, was a good deal larger and immeasurably stronger.

"I think that is enough, sir," he said quietly, but firmly.

Fungy backed down.

"My God, did you see that? He floored Merrick like he was nothing." He heard one onlooker say to another.

"Got a bit out of control there, didn't he?" the second gentleman said.

"Not quite a fair mill. Merrick didn't stand a chance under that onslaught," said another.

They were right. Fungy took a deep breath then turned around and extended his hand down to his cousin.

He was still breathing hard, but the pounding in Fungy's head was beginning to subside. Never before had he ever wanted to hurt anyone as much as he had wanted to hurt Merry. And as he helped his cousin to stand up, he prayed that he never would again.

Merry's face was already beginning to turn black and blue. Sin quickly handed him a handkerchief to stem the trickle of blood that was dripping from his nose.

Fungy walked from the ring and began to dress. He was carefully tying his neckcloth in front of a mirror when Merry came up behind him, still buttoning his waistcoat, and touched him on the shoulder.

"Shall we dine at Whites?"

"Happy to."

For the first time in a while, Fungy felt quite light-hearted, and much more like his old cheery self.

As he walked out with Sin and his cousin, still smiling and joking even through his slightly battered face, Fungy felt a pang of contrition. He wondered for a moment whether he ought to thank his cousin for understanding him so well, and for letting him take out his frustrations on him.

But he kept his own counsel, knowing that the thanks would be more uncomfortable for his cousin than the injuries he had just sustained.

Thirteen

"Who is that, Rose? That is certainly the finest horse I have seen yet," Thalia said, looking ahead to their left, where a black gelding ridden by an straight-backed gentleman was coming toward them.

"I believe that is Lord Hawksmore. He is a duke. I am certain that he would not even look my way."

"Oh."

"What about the gentleman over there, driving that high-perch phaeton with the bright yellow wheels? He is very handsome," Laia said, straining her neck to get a better view.

"Laia, sit properly. You look like you are about to fall off your horse," Rose reprimanded her sister.

Laia shifted herself back into her proper position and frowned at Rose. "Well, I don't see how we can see anybody, with this line moving so very slowly," she complained.

"But that is the way it is in the park at this time of day. If you want to see anyone, you must be patient."

"Oh, look!"

"What, Thalia, is it another handsome horse?" Laia asked, sounding extremely bored.

Thalia whipped her head around and looked like she was about to stick her tongue out at her sister. She refrained, however, and merely said in her haughtiest voice, "It is a very handsome *man*, if you want to know."

"Where?" Laia was instantly very interested, and stretched her neck out once more to see where her sister had been looking.

"Ha! You are only interested in the men."

"Well, that is what we are here for after all—not to look at horses! Rose doesn't want to marry a horse."

"All right, that is enough," Rose said, with as much authority as she could muster through her suppressed laughter.

They had been riding around the park for nearly thirty minutes, tempers shortening as the ride grew longer.

It wasn't even only her sisters whose tiredness affected their tempers; she knew that she, too, was becoming rather downcast. Looking at handsome gentlemen and fine horses was not going to help her to find a rich husband. And she was not entirely sure that this was the best use of her time.

What she needed was another opportunity to play cards. It was the only way out of her current dilemma.

She *had* to win back the vowel she had written to Lord Kirtland. Then she could resume playing to pay off the bills, and only then everything would finally be all right. But just now, it was her debt to Lord Kirtland that was worrying her the most.

Of course, if she married Lord Kirtland the problem would be solved, a little voice in the back of her head reminded her. And it was possible that she could. He did try to kiss her last night.

The salty taste of blood told her that she'd been nibbling too long and too hard at her lip. No one was going to want to kiss her if she kept doing that.

"It's not fair! Thalia is much taller than I am, she can see more," Laia complained, abruptly bringing Rose's mind back to the present.

Rose ignored her and asked, "Thalia, who did you see that you were exclaiming over just a moment ago?"

"It is Fungy, Rose, over there." This time she pointed her finger, despite Rose having told her not to do so numerous times.

Rose did not reprimand her sister again, and just turned. It was indeed Fungy, driving a beautiful bright red phaeton pulled by a very fine looking black horse.

Not to be outdone by his equipage, Fungy himself was wearing a deep green, double-breasted coat, which showed off his broad shoulders and narrow waist. If Rose had not already known that his shoulders and arms were muscular from having seen him without his coat on the day he saved Thalia from the river, his clothing today would have left no doubt to it at all.

"Oh, my," Laia sighed.

Rose echoed the sentiment, but had the presence of mind not to say so out loud.

Then he leaned back, laughing at something, and Rose caught a glimpse of his companion. She felt as if the breath had been taken from her body.

Fungy had invited Miss Halsbury out for a drive!

"Who is that young lady with whom he is driving? Do you know her, Rose?" Thalia asked.

Rose's mind was in a whirl making it difficult to answer her at first, but then she reprimanded herself for her petty jealousy and said, "Harriet Halsbury. She is a very nice girl. I met her at Lady Anson's soiree."

There was no reason why she should be jealous of Miss Halsbury, Rose told herself, sternly sucking the blood from her lip again. She was not interested in Fungy. She was going to marry Lord Kirtland.

That thought stopped her for a moment. Had she actually made up her mind to marry him? She shrugged mentally. She supposed she had.

She then nodded to herself. Yes, she had. She was absolutely right. She *was* going to marry Lord Kirtland. Fungy was just a very kind, and handsome, friend—nothing more.

In fact, she told herself, she was very happy he was out with Miss Halsbury. She liked Miss Halsbury.

"What is he doing driving with her?" Laia asked, peevishly.

"Why should he not?" Rose asked.

"Because he should be out driving with you," Thalia answered for her older sister.

"Yes," Laia concurred.

"No," Rose replied. "He should be out driving with whomever he wants. And clearly, he wants to be with Miss Halsbury." Rose spurred her horse toward Fungy's phaeton. "Come, let's say hello."

Fungy reined in his horse as soon as he saw Rose and her sisters approaching.

"How do you do, Miss Grace, Miss Thalia, Miss Laia," he said, nodding his head to each of the sisters in turn.

"How do you do, Fungy? How nice to see you, Miss Halsbury. It is a lovely day for a ride, is it not?" Rose said, brightly.

"Fungy, it is good to see you again," Laia said warmly.

"How do you do?" Thalia added, nodding to both Fungy and Miss Halsbury.

Rose introduced her younger sisters to Miss Halsbury, who smiled sweetly at them, but said nothing.

"I do hope you haven't had the urge to go swimming again, Miss Thalia?" Fungy asked, smiling at her.

Thalia laughed. "No, sir. I think I shall follow your advice and wait until we go out into the country to do that again."

"Do you enjoy swimming, Miss Thalia?" Miss Halsbury asked with a polite smile.

"Yes, I do, but that is not what Fungy is referring to," she said, giggling.

"Unfortunately, Thalia had a little mishap at the docks the other day and ended up in the river. Fungy was kind enough to help her out again," Rose explained briefly.

"What do you mean, help her out again? You make it sound so tame, Rose," Laia objected. "She fell into the water, Miss Halsbury, and her dress caught on something so that she could not swim back to dock by herself. Fungy was incredibly brave and dove in after her. He nearly drowned in the process of saving her!"

"Oh, my!"

"Miss Laia's version does make it sound much more exciting, but it was nothing, really," Fungy said dismissively. "Glad to see you suffered no ill effects, Miss Thalia."

"None at all. Did you? You seemed to be a little upset by the whole thing," Thalia said, looking at Fungy with concern.

"Thalia!" Rose protested her sister's blunt honesty.

"It is all right, Miss Grace," Fungy said. "I was, indeed, upset by it. Diving into the river is not very pleasant, nor is nearly drowning. However, Miss Thalia, thanks to your eldest sister, I am perfectly well to tell the tale."

Laia and Thalia looked to Rose in surprise, but she had no idea what he was talking about. She was no less shocked by this pronouncement than her sisters seemed to be. "Me? Whatever did I do, sir?"

Fungy looked at her with disconcerting warmth in his eyes. "Why, you called out to me, Miss Grace. It was your sweet voice that called me back from the watery depths."

"Oh." Rose did not know what to say, but for some reason she found herself with a great desire to reach out and take Fungy's hand, or to touch him in some way. Their eyes locked for just the briefest moment, but in that short space of time she knew that he was feeling the same way.

The tingles that she had been thinking about just that morning went rushing through her body. His deep blue, smiling eyes took up her whole world.,

Her horse shifted under her and she was brought back to reality with a jolt.

"You were so long under the water," she stammered by way of explanation. She could feel the stares of both her sisters and Miss Halsbury, and she knew that she must be blushing furiously.

"Ah, well, now my little secret is out, I suppose." Fungy's cheeks turned slightly pink as well. Had he not meant to say such a personal thing?

There was an awkward silence, and then a voice called from behind Fungy's phaeton. "I say, Fungy, are you going to begin moving again or do I have to try and go around you?"

A Dandy In Disguise

A look of relief swept over his face before Fungy turned around and waved at the gentleman behind him. "You will have to excuse us, Miss Grace..." he began.

"Of course," she said, and turned her horse quickly so that she and her sisters could reenter the flow of traffic going the other way. "Good bye. It was very nice seeing you again, Miss Halsbury, you will have to stop by and pay us a visit sometime," she said, just before riding away.

It wasn't that she was anxious to get away from Fungy, she thought as she kicked her horse into a trot, it was simply too embarrassing a situation, and to have had to endure that with her sisters watching... well, she just hoped that they wouldn't question her about it later. And it had nothing to do with her feelings for Fungy. He was simply a friend, she reminded herself firmly, despite the tingles.

Fungy saw Miss Halsbury looking shrewdly at him as they continued on their drive through the park.

He was sure that the ever-perceptive Miss Halsbury knew exactly what was on his mind—why in heaven's name he had told them all that Miss Grace had saved him from drowning.

The problem was that he had no answer whatsoever. He had not wanted to make Miss Grace feel awkward—which she had, of course. He had not wanted Miss Halsbury to feel as if he wanted to be with Miss Grace rather than her—which just might be the truth, but that was not the point.

The point was that he should not have revealed himself in such a way. It was very unlike him to do so. And the look which they shared—it was simply not something one did in public!

"Miss Halsbury, you must excuse my lapse. Cannot imagine what caused me to even mention that Miss Grace had called out to me."

"It is quite obvious why, Fungy," Miss Halsbury said quietly.

"Indeed, no. Not at all what you think. Why, I have rarely enjoyed an afternoon spent in a young lady's company as much as I have enjoyed our time together today."

"That is very kind of you to say..."

"Not just saying it, Miss Halsbury, I truly mean it. You are as delightful as a summer's day, as sweet as the most delicious confection—although thankfully, not sticky at all."

Miss Halsbury laughed, distracted. "You shall soon have me blushing, Fungy."

"Nothing wrong with a little flirtation, Miss Halsbury. Rather expected, I would think."

"Yes, I suppose so, but entirely unnecessary, I assure you." She turned her attention back to the people all around them, with a smile on her lips. Fungy felt as if he'd had a narrow escape.

He stole a glance over at Harriet Halsbury. She was a very pleasant young lady, but definitely not his type. He sensed that she knew that, and therefore did not expect him to woo her. It was a good thing—she deserved better than him.

Miss Grace, on the other hand, was surely the road to his destruction. She caused him to lose control over his carefully constructed persona, to say such ridiculous things as he had done today. With barely a word, she encouraged him to do more and to be more. She had him quoting De La Rochefoucauld, reading Greek, wanting to save her and her sisters from the awkward situations they got themselves into, thinking of things he had not thought of in so long. Things he hadn't thought of since before Georgiana left him and took his heart with her.

And, he realized with a start, that it was more than likely that he needed to spend a little more time getting to know Miss Rose Grace—if he was, in fact, serious about finding a wife.

Fourteen

"Excellent news, Rose," Aunt Farmington said, looking up from her embroidery as the three sisters came into the drawing room after their ride.

There was a beautiful bouquet of white and red roses sitting on the table next to her. Laia rushed over to it immediately.

"Oh! These are gorgeous! Who sent them? Was it Fungy?" she asked, leaning over and inhaling the sweet fragrance.

"How could Fungy have had those delivered so fast?" Thalia asked, genuinely perplexed." We just saw him." Aunt Farmington laughed. "They're not from Fungy. They're from your sister's *other* gentleman, Lord Kirtland. The one she's going to marry... as soon as he comes up to scratch," their aunt added in an undertone.

"Oh," Laia sighed. "How sweet. He must really like you, Rose."

"You're going to marry him?" Thalia asked. "But I like Fungy."

Rose just smiled at her little sister. She liked Fungy too, and his admission at the park had touched something deep within her, but he wasn't wealthy like Lord Kirtland. She silently shoved a deep sadness even deeper. If she couldn't marry for love—and she couldn't, she knew, thanks to their family's financial woes—she would at least marry the wealthiest man she could.

A Dandy In Disguise

"You haven't met Lord Kirtland," Rose pointed out to Thalia. "He's a very pleasant gentleman."

"Pleasant?" Thalia scrunched up her nose as if the word smelled.

"And," their aunt continued in a long suffering tone, "his lordship, who came by in person, I might add, requested that you join him in an expedition to the British Museum tomorrow."

"He was here?" Rose asked.

"He delivered the flowers *in person*?" Laia said at the same time.

They looked at each other. Lord Kirtland's personal touch spoke *volumes* about his intent.

"Yes!" Aunt Farmington was clearly pleased with the effect her statement had had. "Naturally, I told him you would be delighted to join him tomorrow. He'll be picking you up at three."

She had hoped to spend the following afternoon with her sisters, drilling them on deportment. After today, it was clear that they needed some lessons on proper behavior in public places. "I don't..." Rose started.

"You aren't arguing with me," Aunt Farmington said. "If you are serious in pursuing this gentleman, you will not turn down an invitation."

"No, ma'am," Rose answered obediently. She shouldn't, her aunt was right. And, besides, the invitation had already been accepted. She couldn't turn it down now. She would just have to find some other time to tutor her sisters.

Just to remind her as to her duty to her family—as if she could possibly forget— on her dressing table in her room, Rose found another bill from the modiste and a simple note reminding Lord Pemberton–Howe that payment was expected. Her father must have read it and left it there for her.

It hurt that he felt she needed such reminding. She was doing the best she could, as quickly as she could.

She would go to the museum with Lord Kirtland. She would be as sweet and charming as she possibly could. But in the end, it was up to *him* to propose. There was nothing she could do to speed that—except maybe kiss the man when he wanted to kiss her, her traitorous mind said. She squeezed her eyes shut at the memory.

Lord Kirtland was her only hope and she would do what needed to be done—*whatever* needed to be done. And really, he wasn't all that bad — it could be a lot worse! No, Lord Kirtland was young, good-looking and an archeologist. She would most definitely respond favorably if he ever tried to kiss her again.

~

"How wonderful this is, my lord," Rose said, trying hard to contain her enthusiasm. She had forgotten how much she enjoyed ancient Egyptian studies. She'd almost forgotten how much she loved archeology! She'd been so focused on her family and settling into their new life here in London, she hadn't even thought about her own interests for what seemed like the longest time.

"I am so glad you think so, Miss Grace," Lord Kirtland said as he slowly led Rose through the first room of exhibits at the British Museum.

"I have been wanting to come to see the museum ever since we first arrived in London. Unfortunately, I just have not had the chance. I can't tell you how much I appreciate your thoughtful offer to bring me here today."

"It is entirely my pleasure."

"Oh, look!" Rose moved forward eagerly to see a mummy in its coffin.

Lord Kirtland held back a little, but Rose gestured for him to join her at the mummy's side.

"Isn't it fascinating? Just look at how well preserved he is. It just astounds me how the ancient Egyptians learned to embalm a body so that it could last for centuries."

"Indeed."

"My father worked closely with Belzoni in Egypt for a number of years, excavating a tomb. The Egyptians were extraordinarily thoughtful when putting together tombs for the dead. Everything a person might need in order to live comfortably in the afterlife was provided."

"Really? Er, yes, I have heard of such things, of course."

"They included mummified meat, as well as dried fruits, and numerous jars and bowls and even money. Absolutely everything that one needed in order to live."

"They found food with the bodies?" a young man standing next to Rose asked.

"Oh yes. It was believed..."

"Please, my lord, I cannot stand here looking at that thing. Oh, I am feeling decidedly unwell," the young lady on the gentleman's arm complained, while putting a limp hand to her forehead. Indeed, she was looking quite pale.

The man was clearly surprised to see his companion looking this way, and immediately escorted her away to sit down on one of the numerous benches in the hall.

Rose turned back to Lord Kirtland and noticed that he too was looking rather pale.

"Perhaps we should move on," she suggested.

"Yes, I think that would be an excellent idea," he said with obvious relief.

He led the way toward a display of jewelry that had also been found in the tomb. "Now here is something quite fascinating. You ladies always like looking at jewelry, do you not?"

Rose was, in fact, not so interested in the jewelry, but she gave him a little smile and tried to live up to his expectation.

"My word, that must cost thousands of pounds, don't you think, Miss Grace?" Lord Kirtland asked, examining the large gold necklet that had adorned the mummy.

"I really couldn't say." Rose looked back at the young lady and gentleman, who were now sitting and holding hands on a bench on the other side of the room. The young lady seemed to be completely recovered and was giggling over something the gentleman was saying.

She caught Rose's eye and then began laughing in earnest, so much so that she had to cover her mouth with her hand.

Rose could not imagine what she had found to be so amusing in a museum, but turned back to Lord Kirtland, who was now examining a wide gold armband.

"Look at the craftsmanship on this piece, Miss Grace," he said, completely absorbed in his study of the armband.

"Yes, it is quite pretty. Shall we move on?" Rose wanted to see the coffin of the other mummy. "I have heard that the inscriptions on the other coffin are believed to have something to do with the god Osiris."

"Ah, yes. I believe I may have heard something to the effect," Lord Kirtland said, slowly walking away from the jewelry. His steps slowed even more as they approached the second mummy and its coffin.

Rose paused. Looking up into Lord Kirtland's face, she noticed him beginning to pale once again. "If you would prefer, we could just look at the lid." Rose pointed away from the mummy, toward where the lid to the coffin was placed apart for inspection.

"Yes, yes. A much better idea. I, er, wouldn't want you to feel unwell like that other young lady."

"How very thoughtful of you, my lord," Rose said wryly, while trying hard not to smile at Lord Kirtland's obvious cover–up of his own discomfort.

"I do so enjoy looking at the hieroglyphs and imagining what they might mean," she said, looking over the coffin lid.

"Yes, and look at all of the gold! Why, it is amazing," Lord Kirtland said, taking a step back to admire the upper half of the lid, which was entirely covered with the precious metal.

"She looks rather life–like, doesn't she?" Rose said, looking at the face painted at the top.

"Yes. Disturbingly so." Lord Kirtland led Rose away, saying, "I don't believe there was any jewelry associated with this mummy."

"No." Rose was not nearly as disappointed in this as Lord Kirtland seemed to be.

As they moved away from the pieces that interested Rose the most, she began to notice that many of the benches in the museum were occupied by young couples. And what amazed her even more was that they seemed to be completely oblivious to their magnificent surroundings.

Although there were a few older couples and groups of gentlemen wandering around looking at the exhibits, the museum also seemed to be just another place where members of the beau monde went to see and be seen. Men and women wandered the rooms of the museum, looking more at the other patrons than at the magnificent artifacts surrounding them. There were even groups of people just standing around talking — and, from what she could overhear, and Rose was certain that it was not the museum or exhibits that was the main topic of discussion. This was even true in the room that held the famous Elgin marbles.

Just seeing these fantastic sculptures outside of their natural habitat made Rose's blood boil. But she held her tongue. She did not wish to engage in another debate over it with Lord Kirtland, who was clearly a strong proponent of the other side of this argument. But, now, considering that Rose had decided to marry the gentleman, she supposed she ought not to argue with him—even an argument of academic nature could be taken quite personally.

Instead, she commented on all that she saw around her. "It just amazes me that so many people can come here and not even look at the exhibits," she said quietly, so that only Lord Kirtland would hear her.

"Well, it is a social outing to come to the museum," he said. "And most young ladies do not have the same interest in these artifacts as you do."

"Yes, it is a shame, but I see you are quite correct."

"A shame, Miss Grace? Why do you think so?"

"Why? Well, because most of the girls of the *ton* do not seem to have been taught how to think beyond fashion and flirtation, my lord. There is so much more to life than society."

Lord Kirtland stopped and smiled down at Rose. "This is what makes you so very unique, Miss Grace."

A Dandy In Disguise

Rose felt her face heat. In that moment, she could imagine many happy years with Lord Kirtland, rummaging through the dirt and exciting finds of an archaeological expedition. What a happy life that would be!

Nothing at all like the mindless meaninglessness of English society. Fungy, despite his kindness, was merely a reflection of that society. He was just as taken up by vagaries of fashion as the silly women who sat about all day gossiping over their tea.

How happy Rose was to have found Lord Kirtland. He was a true intellectual—and even better, a wealthy one.

Fifteen

Fungy resisted the urge to take out his handkerchief and press it to his nose. The combined smell of liquor, smoke, and nervous men was almost too much. But he had to be here. He really did not have any choice in the matter. He supposed that this is what it smelled like to work.

This was the smell of responsibility.

It wasn't that Fungy had never been in a gambling hell before. It was simply that he had no love of gambling, outside of the occasional rubber of whist with his friends, much preferring the overly perfumed smell of a ballroom to this.

But Lord Halsbury was expecting a preliminary report tomorrow morning on his investigation into this gambling scheme, and so far, Fungy had nothing to tell him.

Hopefully something would turn up tonight, in this foul–smelling place.

The problem was that he had absolutely no idea what he was doing. There was nothing much one could discern from just watching others play. And yet, what else could he do?

Fungy sighed, once again casting his keen eyes over the proceedings. Well, one thing was for certain, gentlemen who came to gaming hells did not take as much time over their toilettes as they should. He counted at least six horrendously tied neck cloths. And there were at least seven or eight gentlemen who had worn waistcoats that did not match either their coats or their pantaloons. There were even a few gentlemen in breeches!

Fungy forced himself to stop looking at the men's clothing and concentrate instead on the games they were playing. Who was losing to whom? There had to be some telltale sign that would point toward someone who was cheating.

He moved slowly around the room of the gambling hell, where the sound of coins clinking together intermingled with the men's voices.

Pausing for a few minutes at one table to watch a card game, he caught the eye of a woman of evidently dubious morals. She rubbed herself suggestively against the back of the man sitting directly in front of her, but her eyes were on Fungy.

He quickly broke his gaze and moved on, avoiding that table.

Thinking back to the letter Lord Halsbury had shown him, he tried to remember some of the names listed there. Were any of those people here tonight?

He caught sight of Jack Abbey, the Duke of Hawksmore's cousin and heir. His name had been on the list. And sitting at another table not far away was George Cole, Lord Chester's youngest son. His name had been there, too. There was no way that Fungy could watch both men. Randomly, he picked Abbey.

Abbey was playing with Pip Haston, his cousin Hawksmore and Charles Bradmore. All three men were well known to Fungy, and he could not imagine any one of them leading a gambling ring. But then he remembered the initials at the bottom of the letter—P.H.

Hawksmore? No, his given name was Dominic.

Pip Haston?

Fungy began to watch the game more intently, moving around to stand near enough to Haston so that he could see if he was doing anything unusual.

Haston was a dandy of the first order. A true imitator of Fungy's style, who then took it up one notch. There was something ingenuous about the young man, Fungy had always thought — but perhaps he was being hypocritical. Perhaps there was more there than met the eye.

"I say, see Lady Margaret last night at the Peyton's? Smashing gown she had on, what?" Haston said, as he placed a card on the table.

Bradmore laughed. "Barely had on, don't you mean? Her dresses are getting more daring by the week—soon there will be no top to them at all!"

"Think she's getting a little desperate?" Hawksmore laughed and played his card. For a duke, he was remarkably easygoing. He would be a stunning catch for a girl like Lady Margaret, or for any young lady—not bad to look at and a remarkably nice fellow.

"I'd be interested if her father were a little less exacting in wanting a title," Pip said in a good-natured way as he lost the trick.

"Would you woo her, Jack?" Hawksmore asked, as he placed the first card down on the table for the next trick.

"Who, me? With Lady Margaret? You must be kidding, coz. She's sweet, but nothing in the attic." Abbey played a trump. To be honest, he was actually just the sort Fungy would like to see with Lady Margaret. Such an upright, almost staid young man paired with her flamboyance would no doubt cause some interesting sparks.

"Thought you liked that sort," Bradmore said.

Haston also put down a trump, but it was lower than Abbey's. Fungy didn't quite see the point of that. It was either all he had, or he was deliberately trying to lose.

"No, thank you. I think I shall leave her for some other lucky fellow. Not in the petticoat line just yet, anyway." Abbey began to pick up the cards on the table one by one, having won the trick.

"Oh, damn! Didn't mean to put down that card," Haston exclaimed as he watched Abbey pick up his card.

The men laughed. No, there could be no possibility that Pip Haston was the man Fungy was looking for.

"Fungy! What are you doing here?" Merry said, slapping him on the back and making Fungy jump. The men at the table all turned to look up at him.

"Fungy, didn't see you standing there. Been there long?" Haston asked.

"Oh, er, no, not long. Do better to watch what you put down, Haston. Getting yourself distracted with your own chatter."

Fungy laughed as the other men at the table did as well.

"That's why we like to play with him," Hawksmore said.

Haston had the grace to blush, but hid it by taking a long sip from his brandy. "Not very good at this," he said sheepishly, when he had put down his glass.

"So what are you doing here?" Merry said to Fungy again. With some relief, Fungy noticed that his cousin's handsome, friendly face had healed completely from their boxing match.

"Don't believe I've ever seen you in a gaming hell before," Sin, who was standing just behind Merry, added.

"Oh, just thought I'd stop in and watch a bit before heading off to Lady Roseberry's ball." Fungy shrugged. He then pulled out his watch and took a look at the time.

It was nearly ten–thirty. Not too late to drop in on the ball. He was a little worried that whoever it was he was looking for wouldn't be here for another few hours. Now that he'd committed himself, he had no choice but to abandon his search for the evening.

"Don't mean to scare you off," Merry said.

"Yes, why don't you stay and play a rubber with us?" Sin asked. After having given up playing cards for many years, he had recently begun to play again, but now with much more control than in his salad days. He'd had the unfortunate experience of accidentally bankrupting a family when he'd won their estate in a game of cards. Of course, it had all worked out for the best—he was now very happily married to the granddaughter of the fellow from whom he won the property.

"Not sure I have the time. Should really get over to Lady Roseberry's. Hadn't meant to stay this long as it is," Fungy said. He then took himself off before anyone could say anything.

Whew! That was close. He would have to watch himself more closely. He couldn't risk anyone—not even his closest friends—finding out what he was doing. He'd promised Lord Halsbury that he would disclose his occupation to no one.

Of course, now he would have no information to disclose to Lord Halsbury either.

Fungy hailed a hackney and directed the driver to the Roseberry's.

A Dandy In Disguise

Well, at least he had eliminated one person with the initials P.H. Were there any others that he knew of? Fungy ran through a mental list of all the people he knew, searching for someone with those particular initials.

The only one he could come up with was Lord Pemberton–Howe, Miss Grace's father. But that was impossible. He wasn't the gambling sort, though Fungy supposed he was intelligent enough to organize such a thing.

Fungy wondered what his finances were like. He had to have spent a great deal of money on his expeditions. Could it be that he was desperate for cash—so desperate that he would hire people to cheat at cards for him?

No. Fungy just could not see Lord Pemberton–Howe in that role. Besides, Miss Grace and her sisters were all very well dressed. If he were in financial straits, it was unlikely that he would spend the money necessary to dress his daughters so well.

That meant that there had to be somebody else.

Rose had just sat down with her sisters in the drawing room for the belated lesson on proper behavior when a maid rushed into the room, immediately followed by Fungy.

The maid, unaware that Fungy was just behind her, curtseyed. "Miss, there's a gentleman here who says that it's urgent..."

"Thank you, I think I'll just tell her myself," Fungy interrupted the maid with a smile that would have charmed even the highest stickler in society.

The maid started, then ran from the room, giggling.

Rose stood up. "Fungy, what a lovely surprise."

"Thank you. I do hope I'm not interrupting something, but I fear that I must whisk you away from your sisters for a short time. There is some incredibly important news that has just come and the archaeological society is holding an emergency meeting right now."

Chills of excitement sped through Rose. She'd never heard Fungy speak with such thrill in his voice. His usual façade of ennui had completely disappeared. This must be serious, indeed! "What is it? Does my father know?"

"He is waiting for us downstairs," Fungy said with a nod.

Rose hesitated, turning towards her sisters. "It's fine, Rose, you go on," Laia said.

"Absolutely! You must go. Clearly, this is much more important," Thalia agreed. , standing up, and even beginning to physically push Rose toward the door.

Rose was not fooled. Not for an instant. She stopped and turned on both girls, putting her hands on her waist. "If you think I will let this..." she waved her hand in the air, "whatever it is, distract me from giving you two this lesson, you can think again."

"You certainly must give your sisters whatever lesson you were planning, but surely it's something that can wait?" Fungy asked, giving the two girls a broad, conspiratorial smile.

"Yes, it is," Laia agreed. Thalia nodded her head vigorously, sending her braids flying.

Rose didn't like leaving her sisters again, but clearly whatever was going on at the archaeological society was something of great importance. She just couldn't be left out—especially not after her visit to the British Museum the previous day had reminded her so

A Dandy In Disguise

strongly of her love of archeology and all that she'd missed since they'd come to London. But she had a responsibility to her sisters, a little voice inside of her argued. Archeology wasn't going to get her married or the bills paid.

"I'm sorry, Fungy..." she started to say.

He stopped her, taking her hand in his own. "Miss Grace, your devotion to your sisters is admirable and I'm certain that they appreciate all that you do for them, but I think you can afford to take a little time for yourself. Just an hour, perhaps two. That's all that I'm asking." His blue eyes looked into her own, pleading with her. His smile enticing her to throw her responsibilities out the window.

Even her sisters were looking at her with hopeful eyes. How could she say no when they were all ganging up on her like this?

Rose sighed. "Very well. But this does not mean that I'm going to forget about this lesson." She wagged her finger at her sisters.

"We'll even remind you of it," Laia said, taking up pushing her toward the door where Thalia had left off.

As they walked down the stairs to join her father, Rose finally asked, "So what is the excitement that has caused this emergency meeting?"

"A letter has just arrived from Lady Hester Stanhope. She's made some startling new discoveries in the Holy Land. Being a lady archeologist yourself, I was certain you'd be eager to hear of her travails."

Rose's heart sped up at the thought—a woman archeologist, out on her own, doing research and conducting her own digs. She reached out and put her hand on Fungy's shoulder. He stopped mid-way down the stairs and turned to look up at her. "Thank you." The words and the sentiment came from deep within her, even she was a little startled at their intensity.

Fungy took her hand from his shoulder and pressed a kiss to her fingertips. "It is entirely my pleasure, I assure you."

Her father cleared his throat from just below them. "Shall we get a move on, then? I don't want to be left standing in the back of the room."

Rose could feel the heat of her blush from her head straight down to her toes, but she and Fungy turned and hurried the rest of the way down the stairs.

Sixteen

The talk was everything Rose could have hoped for. It was fascinating from both a general intellectual standpoint and an archaeological one. Rose loved hearing all that Lady Stanhope had endured on her journey to the Holy Land, even though it made her pine for her days out in the field.

It was odd that Lord Kirtland hadn't been there, however. When Rose, Fungy and her father had first gone in, and when they exited after the talk, she'd looked about for him, but he was nowhere to be seen. She didn't say a word to either of her escorts, however, not believing that it would be polite to do so.

"Would you care to join me for a cup of coffee?" Fungy asked Rose and her father as they stood waiting for her father's carriage.

"I would love to," Rose answered.

"Not for me, thank you," Lord Pemberton–Howe said at nearly the same time. "I've got work to do. This has been very exciting, but I don't think I should take even more time away from my own work. But you two go on and have a good time." He stepped out into the street and waved down a hackney before Rose could object, and was gone.

Fungy took her to a nearby shop where they spent a happy hour discussing Lady Stanhope's letter and her findings in detail before—.

"Fungy!" A finely dressed gentleman with blond hair that slipped into his eyes stopped by their table.

"Oh, hello, Merry," Fungy drawled, suddenly reverting back to his usual slow speech. It was such an abrupt change, Rose had to stifle the urge not to laugh at his affectation.

He turned to Rose. "Miss Grace, may I present my cousin, the Marquis of Merrick. Merry, Miss Rose Grace."

Rose shook hands with the gentleman. "It's a pleasure."

The man was looking at Fungy curiously, so he explained, "Miss Grace and I have just attended an emergency meeting of the archaeological society. A letter arrived from Lady Stanhope in the Holy Land."

"Really?" The man's eyes couldn't possibly get any wider or his eyebrows any higher up on his forehead.

Fungy seemed to enjoy the fact that he'd shocked his cousin, for he laughed a little and patted his shoulder, but didn't say anything.

Rose and Fungy had been so engrossed in their conversation that she only noticed now did that most of the little tables scattered around the shop were empty. "I should probably return home," she told Fungy, who stood up immediately.

"Of course. I did promise to return you to your sisters, didn't I?"

Rose laughed. "Yes, although I'm certain they they'd be very happy for me to stay gone. I was about to embark on a lesson in deportment."

"Younger sisters, I presume?" Lord Merrick asked.

Rose laughed. "Yes. And I have to say, sir, your cousin has been an excellent influence on them. They were actually willing to sit through my lesson thanks to him, whereas only a month ago, my mention of the subject would have sent them running."

"Really?" The gentleman seemed as shocked by this as he had been at the fact that Fungy had been attending a lecture. He looked at Fungy, assessment in his eyes.

Fungy just shrugged. "I would hate to disappoint your sisters, in that case. Shall we?"

"Thank you. It was very nice meeting you, my lord," Rose said to Fungy's cousin.

"It has been enlightening, Miss Grace," his lordship said with an small bow.

※

Lord Kirtland held out his arm for Rose to take after the orchestra had played the final notes of the country dance. Rose was certain that there would soon be talk, for that was the third time she and Lord Kirtland had danced together that evening.

She tried to hide the silly smile that had plagued her all through the dance.

Lord Kirtland was certain to ask her to marry him. There was absolutely no doubt about that, not now. Not after asking her to dance three times.

She had been happy when he'd asked her to dance a second time, since that meant that he truly was interested in her. But a *third* time? Well, there could be no clearer indication of his intentions.

"I do hope you will excuse me, Miss Grace," Lord Kirtland said, breaking into her thoughts as he returned her to her aunt.

Rose nodded, flashing him a bright smile, and then watched him make his way directly for the card room.

She sighed happily. Despite her sisters' protestations that Fungy was the man for her, Rose still believed firmly that she could not have found a more perfect gentleman to marry than Lord Kirtland.

She wondered how he was going to propose. Would he visit her and then get down on one knee in front of her? Would he take her for a moonlit walk through a lovely rose garden? Or perhaps he would take her for another romantic tour of the British Museum? Only, this time it would be her sitting on a bench, oblivious to her surroundings, as Lord Kirtland whispered words of love in her ear and asked her to spend the rest of her life with him.

"Good evening, Miss Grace," Rose heard beside her. She shook off her thoughts and looked beside her to find Fungy smiling warmly at her. "You look lovely in that particular shade of pink. Should definitely wear such colors more often."

"Oh, Fungy! How do you do?" Rose laughed with embarrassment at having been caught in her fantasies. "I am afraid I was wool-gathering and didn't see you approach."

He was looking quite magnificent in a coat of dark green superfine and cream–colored pantaloons. His neckcloth flowed down into his waistcoat in what Rose thought must be what was called a waterfall. His waistcoat was cream, shot with gold with a lovely green floral pattern. Complete, as ever, to a shade.

"Seemed to be thinking of something very pleasant, by the smile you had on your face."

Rose felt her face heat. "Did I? Oh, how very silly of me!"

"Almost hate to tear you away from your happy thoughts, but wondered if you might grant me the next dance?"

"I would be honored, sir," she said quickly, to cover up her embarrassment.

But then, to Rose's dismay, the orchestra began playing the introductory chords for a waltz. Dancing such an intimate dance with Fungy, just after her three dances with Lord Kirtland, somehow seemed... awkward, almost like a betrayal. But she did not have a good excuse to sit it out either, as she'd recently been granted permission to dance the waltz by the lady patronesses of Almack's. She had no choice but to take Fungy's hand, and then to allow him to place his other hand on the small of her back.

Luscious tingles shot through her body at his touch, and her mind immediately shot to the wonderful afternoon she'd spent with him just the day before.

How was it that she always got these odd sensations when Fungy touched her, and such different feelings when it was Lord Kirtland?

She looked up into Fungy's eyes. He looked so happy to be with her! The now–familiar feeling of being comfortable and warm swept over her. What was it about this man that made her feel so safe and cared for when she was with him?

It was nearly the opposite feeling from that which Lord Kirtland inspired, but it was his lordship who she was going to marry. And he had many other wonderful qualities, she reminded herself.

Even if he never made her feel like this.

Fungy's lips were turned up in a small smile, and his eyes held hers in what felt like a loving embrace. He looked like he could happily stay this way for the rest of his life.

Oh, but so could she.

But she must not, her mind screamed to her. She was going to marry Lord Kirtland. She should not be feeling this way.

Yet, the heat of Fungy's body was so close to hers—warming her, enveloping her, protecting her. She felt so good, so feminine, and so very happy.

Rose tried to fight the feelings, tried to turn her eyes away from his, and found it impossible.

She was lost. Lost in his eyes. Lost in his presence. Lost in *him*. And slowly, she let her thoughts flutter away as they danced.

He twirled her around the room, moving gracefully to the music, but Rose hardly noticed. They did not speak a word to each other, but it didn't matter. No words were necessary. Everything that they felt, everything that they needed to convey to the other, was there in their eyes. They understood each other. They felt the same thing—this utter wonderfulness of just being close to each other, of moving together as one.

A silence fell heavily all around them, suddenly. Rose was reluctantly roused from her blissful state. Had the music stopped?

Surely it had happened too quickly. What had happened to the dance? It seemed much too soon for it to be over.

Fungy took a step back and bowed to her. Purely through instinct, Rose returned it with her own curtsy. Her head felt like it was in a fog. She wasn't entirely sure where she was, or what she should be doing.

Luckily, Fungy was there. Without a word, he gently placed his hand on the small of her back sending a lovely heat up her spine. He led her outside onto the balcony. The fresh air and heady fragrance from the garden below awoke Rose abruptly to the reality of her situation.

She had just shared the most romantic dance she ever had danced, with *Fungy*!

She had never thought of him as romantic before. In fact, quite the opposite. He was warm and comfortable. He was her friend.

And... he was not someone with whom she should be sharing such feelings. It was wrong. She was going to marry Lord Kirtland.

Fungy leaned against the balustrade next to her, but Rose didn't look at him. She didn't need to. She could feel him. He wasn't nearly as close to her as he had been while they were dancing, but she could still feel his presence, still smell his musky cologne and hear the rustle of his coat.

She had never been so intensely aware of anyone before.

But what about Lord Kirtland? He had danced with her three times. She had made up her mind to marry him—and if she didn't after tonight, she would doubtless be labeled a loose–skirt, or worse.

But she couldn't ignore Fungy, either. Finally, she forced herself to turn to him, intent on saying something that would indicate that their waltz had been a mistake, or to make some sort of joke about how she had completely lost herself in his arms.

But the words died on her lips. He was looking at her with such a confused expression on his face that she nearly laughed. It was such a relief to see that he was as puzzled by what had just happened as she was.

"Rose... Miss Grace..." he began, when Aunt Farmington's voice intruded abruptly.

"Rose, you should not be out here alone, my girl!"

Rose felt her face heat, and spun around to address her aunt.

"We were, er..." she stammered.

"Just getting some fresh air, ma'am. After the exertion of the dance, Miss Grace felt the need for a breath of air." With Lady Farmington, it seemed, Fungy had no problems finding his voice, and he took command of the situation with his usual aplomb.

"Yes, that's it. Nothing beyond that, Aunt Farmington, truly," Rose said gratefully.

"Ah, then you won't mind if I join you? It is quite a pleasant evening, isn't it? A little warm for this time of year, though," Aunt Farmington said, stepping in between Rose and Fungy.

They moved farther apart to allow her room, exchanging a quick glance. There was something that had needed to be said, but it would have to wait.

"Yes, it has been quite unseasonably warm," Fungy agreed.

"It makes it quite comfortable to wear these thin dresses that are all the rage, without the need for a shawl," the older lady said, rubbing one bare arm with her gloved hand.

"Are you chilled, ma'am? Shall I call someone to fetch your shawl?" Fungy asked.

Aunt Farmington narrowed her eyes at him, and then turned her intent scrutiny on Rose before answering. "No. No, I thank you. I shall send someone for it, and to find your father, Rose. I believe it is time we went home. You will join me in the foyer within five minutes."

"Yes, Aunt Farmington," Rose answered. Her aunt nodded curtly and left them alone once more on the balcony.

She then gave an embarrassed laugh. "She is turning into an excellent chaperone. She wasn't quite up to it when we first arrived, but now she is becoming quite the dragon."

Fungy gave a laugh. "I believe she sees more than you may realize. Older ladies have quite a talent for that."

An awkward silence hung between them for a moment. Somehow, the moment had passed, and Rose did not know how to bring it back.

"Well, goodnight," Fungy said at the same time as she said, "I should be going."

They both gave an embarrassed laugh, and Rose turned and walked away.

Fungy watched her go with a greater feeling of loss than he had ever experienced after saying goodnight to a young lady. He could not imagine what was getting into him.

First, he had been so amazingly inept at saying anything while they had danced, and then had not even been able to alleviate the awkward silence that had continued afterward.

But was it awkward? It had not seemed so during the dance. It had seemed right. Everything about that dance had seemed right.

It hadn't been, though, not in the least. Fungy shook his head. It had felt so right, but even that was wrong.

It shouldn't have felt so good. It shouldn't have happened at all. He was in love with Georgiana. She had held his heart for over fifteen years; how could he just throw that away now?

He couldn't. He wouldn't! No matter what. He would pay Miss Grace a visit the very next day and apologize to her. Yes. That's what he needed to do. Apologize and promise that nothing like that would ever, ever...

Oh, but he wished it would. She'd felt so good, so right...

No!

Fungy gave himself a shake, took a few deep cooling breaths of the heavily scented air, and pointed himself in the direction of the ballroom. There were many more proper young ladies there, with whom he should dance.

But none of them would be Rose.

Seventeen

Fungy stopped for a moment at the edge of the ballroom. He looked around at all of the hopeful young ladies who lined the walls, each standing next to their equally hopeful mamas.

They all looked so... uninteresting.

It would take a great deal of willpower to ask any one of them to dance tonight. After the waltz he had shared with Miss Grace, any other young woman would seem insipid.

"A true gentleman would not just stand by without asking a lady to dance, St. John," a soft, familiar voice said just behind him.

Fungy felt his heart stop. He turned around and fifteen years of his life slipped away.

Georgiana stood just behind him.

She looked, if possible, even more beautiful than Fungy remembered. Her thick chestnut hair gleamed with luster in the candlelight, just a few tendrils allowed to surround her lovely face. Brown smiling eyes laughed at him, as did her full pink lips.

He took a step closer, feeling as if he was lost in a dream. Her familiar scent, a musky rose, wafted over him like a warm summer day.

"Well? Will you not ask me to dance? Do I need to be so bold as to ask you?" she said, still laughing at him.

Fungy pulled himself together and made her a grand leg. "I would be grateful if you would honor me with this dance, my lady."

Her low chuckle washed over him as she held out her hand for him to take.

Gracefully, he swept her into his arms, thrilled that the orchestra was playing another waltz. Even after all these years, she felt as familiar to him as any woman could.

And yet there was something missing as he held her.

He studied her face as she smiled up at him. There was perhaps a wrinkle or two that had not been there the last time he'd seen her, but other than that she was exactly the same.

So what had changed?

As he gently turned her about the room, he realized that it wasn't her, it was him. There was no tingle, no spark, no automatic tightening of his loins that he'd always felt whenever he'd seen her or held her. It just wasn't there. There was no sexual appeal, no feeling of anticipation, no thrill.

But how could this be? He couldn't be still thinking about Rose.

But that must be it. Yet how could he be thinking of her when he had Georgiana, *his Georgiana,* back in his arms? It used to be that he couldn't think of another woman when he was with her. In fact, for so many years he'd not been able to think of any other woman at all. And yet, here he was, with no romantic feelings for her whatsoever—this woman who had been his entire life and love.

Fungy's instinctive manners rescued him from revealing his sudden shocking discovery. He smiled down at her expectant face.

"Haven't changed, Georgiana. Not a bit."

"Tsk," she waved aside his compliment. "But you have, St. John." She moved back a bit in his arms and looked him over. "You are complete to a shade."

Fungy bowed his head. "Thank you."

"And from what I hear, you are quite the buck. Dictating fashions, setting all the girls atwitter with your attention, even getting the nod from the matrons. Quite well respected among the gentleman, too."

"Please, making me blush," Fungy said. He was a little embarrassed, but secretly thrilled she'd noticed. He felt like a student who had just received top marks in the class and had his work displayed for everyone to see—but the feeling was as platonic as that, as well.

"I've simply made myself into the man you wanted, Georgiana," Fungy said quietly, after a moment to regain control of his pride.

Georgiana's eyes opened wide at this. "The man *I* wanted?"

"Told me so the last day we were together. Said that you were marrying Mirthwood because I was not fashionable enough for you, not a member of the *haute ton.*"

Georgiana thought about this, clearly dredging up the old memory. "I did, didn't I?"

"So, you see before you the man you wanted me to be."

She smiled at him, but the look in her eye was sad, as if she had lost something dear to her.

"How is Mirthwood?" Fungy asked, wondering what she was doing here. Why wasn't she still in America with her husband? the dialogue tag needing a second half.

Georgiana glanced up at that. "Have you not heard?" At his questioning look, she continued, "He died last year. The doctors believe it was cancer, but they couldn't be sure."

"I am terribly sorry."

Georgiana gave a gentle nod, then shrugged, a little half–smile on her lips. "So here I am. Back in London, returned to the bosom of society. Once again a widow, wondering if I want to try fate and marriage a third time."

Eighteen

The words were at the tip of his tongue: Why don't you marry me, Georgiana? But they wouldn't come out.

At one time, he would have said it in a trice. He would have said it without having to think about it even for a moment. But now he just could not make himself say the words, could not make himself feel the love and the passion for her he had once felt.

The dance ended. Georgiana took Fungy's arm, and he led her out onto the balcony where he had just been with Miss Grace.

Georgiana leaned out looking into the garden below. "So, who is this young woman to whom you have given your heart?"

Fungy felt a rush of sheer shock run through him. But he made himself turn casually to look at her, leaning one hip against the balustrade. "Don't know what you mean."

She gave him a sly little smile. "Oh, come now, St. John. You need not be coy with me. I can tell. What is her name?"

"If you mean Miss Grace, I assure you—"

"Oh, please, St. John. If you begin to lie to me and take on these airs, I will simply wash my hands of you," she said, standing up and moving away from him.

Fungy turned toward the garden and leaned his hands on the railing. "Don't know that you could exactly call it love…"

"From the look I saw the two of you share while you danced, I would say it was." She tapped his arm. "I know. I used to receive those looks too."

Fungy snapped his head back to look at her, but she didn't look sad or upset. In fact, she looked happy—happy for him.

But was she right? Was he, in fact, in love with Miss Grace? Was that what those feelings had been? But he couldn't be. He was in love with Georgiana—or at least, he had been.

She nodded and rested her hand gently on his sleeve. "It is all right, St. John. I believe it has been long enough, if not too long." She took a step away from him. "I must say, I was truly surprised to hear that you hadn't married. But perhaps you were just waiting for the right young lady? And now, I take it, you believe this Miss Grace is the one worthy enough?"

Fungy gave a little laugh. "She is more than worthy. I wonder if I am worthy enough for her. But as for love…"

"St. John! Do not tell me you weren't aware of your feelings?"

Fungy stood silently, looking at Georgiana. She had always been so perceptive, such an excellent judge of character, and of his in particular. He supposed that if she thought that he was in love with Miss Grace, it must be so. And, in fact, the more he thought about it, the more he thought that she might just be right.

Those feelings… losing himself with her as they had danced… He thought about it for a moment and then decided, that, yes, he *did* love Miss Grace. He'd tried to tell himself otherwise, tried to remind himself that he was in love with Georgiana. But now that his first love was here at hand, he realized with a deep sadness—somewhere, sometime, he'd fallen out of love with Georgiana.

"Tell me more about her," Georgiana demanded.

Fungy shrugged. "She is... sweet and innocent, and extremely intelligent. She is the daughter of Lord Pemberton–Howe, the archaeologist."

Georgiana burst out laughing. "An archaeologist! Why that is perfect for you, St. John. Couldn't be any better. Perhaps *she* will understand your funny classical quotes."

Fungy laughed. "Yes, I believe she would. Not only that, but she would know who said them and would have read them herself, in the original Greek."

"Oh, St. John. I am so happy for you. And I'm certain that with a girl like that you don't need all this." She indicated his clothes. "I'm sure that she loves you just as you are."

Fungy lost his smile. "I don't know that she loves me at all. I've never shown her who I truly am. To her, I am merely Fungy and a dandy."

"But surely you've quoted your sayings to her? She knows that you enjoy all of those classical books you are forever reading?"

Fungy shook his head. "No, Georgiana. I stopped reading them for a while. In fact, it was meeting Miss Grace that inspired me to pick them up again."

He paused and then added quietly, "I think even my closest friends have forgotten who I truly am."

Georgiana placed her hand on his arm. "I am sorry. But you should not let this stop you from pursuing this young lady. *Show* her who you are. Let her meet St.

John—the real you. You know she will love you for it. Unlike silly women like me, she will appreciate not only your physical beauty, but the beauty of your mind as well."

"I..."

"You know that you love her, and I know that she sounds absolutely perfect for you. What are you waiting for?"

"For you," he whispered, his voice not quite working. "I was waiting for you, Georgiana. Whether you meant to or not, you did take my heart with you when you left."

She gave him a little smile, her eyes beginning to shine with tears. "Then let me give it back to you, St. John so that you may give it to Miss Grace."

He nodded, and then took his old love in his arms, feeling her supple curves against his body, knowing that he felt nothing for her.

No, that wasn't true—he felt for her the greatest respect, and friendship. But his heart was his own, again, and free to give to another.

As she slowly came awake, Rose could feel the presence of others on her bed. She could feel their excitement, their anticipation — their bouncing.

She cracked one eye open, saw Thalia's face within inches of her own, and immediately squeezed her eye shut again.

"I saw that!" Thalia said.

Rose turned over, and came face to face with Laia, who was resting her elbow on Rose's pillow, watching her. She was surrounded.

She turned onto her stomach and buried her head in her pillow.

"You can't hide from us, Rose. Time for your report," Thalia sang into her ear.

Rose lifted her pillow to hide her head under, but it was snatched from her hands before she could do so.

"Oh no, you don't. We want to know about the ball last night."

"C'mon Rose, tell us. Did you dance with Fungy?"

"Did you dance with Lord Kirtland?"

"Were you the most fashionably dressed girl there?"

"Does Lord Kirtland play any sport, did you find out?"

"Were there any other interesting gentlemen, perhaps a little younger, who might be interested in a girl not quite out yet?"

Rose groaned and threw her arm over her face. "Why can't you two at least wait until I've woken up before barraging me with questions?"

"That wouldn't be any fun," Thalia objected.

"And we want to know now," Laia added. "If we let you wake up, you might forget to tell us later. And, besides, Aunt Farmington will be in the drawing room later, so you won't be able to give us any of the fun details, like how many times you danced with Fungy." She sat up and crossed her legs in front of her, placing Rose's pillow across her lap.

Rose snatched her pillow back. Putting it behind her, she sat up and leaned back against it.

"Well, did you dance with Lord Kirtland?" Laia asked once again, with great expectation on her face.

Rose smiled at her sister, unable to hide her pleasure. "I did. We danced *three* times."

"Three times? Is that a lot?" Thalia asked.

"Yes, it is. It means he's serious about wanting to marry me. Only people who are engaged or married dance together so many times."

"Are you engaged to him?" Thalia asked.

"No. But I think I might be soon. He needs only to ask."

"But what about Fungy?" Laia asked.

"When do you think he will ask you?" Thalia asked at the same time.

"I don't know when he'll ask," Rose answered her youngest sister. "And Fungy is just a friend, Laia, I've explained that to you already."

Deliberately, she turned her mind away from her memories of the dance they had shared together. That dance had no place in her current plans.

"But I thought you liked him."

"I do like him. I like him very much." Rose slipped past her sisters and got out of bed.

"So you should marry Fungy! Why don't you marry him?" Laia said, snatching the pillow back again and holding it close to her.

Rose picked up her wrapper and put it on, briefly allowing herself to think about Fungy. He'd made her feel good last night. Very good. She had never felt more comfortable and happy with anyone. She could still feel the sensations from the magic they'd shared during their dance.

Magic. Yes, that was it. A few moments' enchantment.

But it was Lord Kirtland who would provide the opportunity for her to work in Egypt and Greece for the rest of her life, as well as provide the money her family desperately needed right now. That is what she needed — not a moment's enchantment, but the security for a lifetime.

She turned around and faced her sisters. "Fungy is a good friend and I care for him a great deal. I feel the same for him as I do for the two of you. In fact, more—he's not as annoying as you two are."

Thalia laughed.

"But that is what makes him perfect," Laia said.

"Just imagine how much fun we would all have together," Thalia agreed brightly.

It was true, Rose thought for a moment. They would all have a grand time together.

But there was more to marriage than just a grand time. She shook her head. "Fungy doesn't make me feel the same way that Lord Kirtland does."

"How does Lord Kirtland make you feel, Rose?" Laia asked.

Rose shrugged and smiled. "All shivery and nervous. With Fungy, I only feel comfortable. He makes me feel good, but he doesn't put me on edge like Lord Kirtland does. I'm certain I'm in love with Lord Kirtland, and nothing more than good friends with Fungy. And besides, Lord Kirtland has so much more to recommend him as a husband—he's rich and an archaeologist, besides being quite handsome."

Laia sighed, but shrugged as if resigning herself to Rose's decision. "Well, then, how are you going to get him to propose?"

Rose sat down on the edge of her bed. "I don't know. I really have no idea what else I can do to let him know I would be open to a proposal. I danced with him three times in one night, I've gone on an outing with him..." Rose shrugged. "What else can I do?"

"You could ask Fungy," Thalia suggested. "I bet he would know." Both Rose and Laia turned to look at their youngest sister. "No!" said Rose at the same time that Laia said, "That is the worst idea I have ever heard."

"Why? I'm sure he would know what Rose needs to do to get Lord Kirtland to propose."

"I could *never* ask Fungy!"

"But you just said what a good friend he was. If he's such a good friend, why can't you ask him?"

Rose thought about this for a minute. Thalia did have a point there. And she was certainly right in that he would know what to do. "I still don't like it. It's not proper." She shook her head and then began to get up.

"Well, if you don't ask him, then I will," Thalia said, crossing her arms over her chest.

"Thalia!"

"Thalia, you wouldn't!" Rose protested.

"Oh yes, I would. He's coming today. He sent 'round a note asking if you would be at home. I believe that Aunt Farmington answered it already, saying that you would be."

Rose gasped. Fungy was coming to pay her a visit? Why? She hoped it wouldn't have anything to do with what had been left unsaid after their dance. "I will speak with him then, but I will *not* ask him how to bring Lord Kirtland up to scratch."

Nineteen

A knock sounded on Rose's door.

She quickly finished tying her wrapper as her father came into the room. He didn't look as if he had slept much the previous night, but there was an odd light in his eyes nonetheless.

"Ah, you all here? Good."

"Good morning, Papa," the three girls said in unison.

He gave them a smile. "Good morning, my three graces." He patted Rose on the cheek. "I have to go out of town for a few days, Rosebud. You will please look after your sisters?"

"Where are you going?" Thalia asked.

"I always look after them, Papa," Rose said.

"Eh? Oh, I've got to go to Pemberton. Ran into our old neighbor Squire Thompson last night at Whites. He told me an interesting bit of news."

He smiled distractedly. "Aunt Farmington will be here, of course. I don't know when I'll be back. Be good," he added sternly to his two younger daughters.

And then before they could ask any more questions, he left.

The three girls just looked at each other.

"I don't believe I've seen him so excited since we were in Greece," Rose said finally.

"Is that what that was, excitement?" Thalia asked.

"He looked very tired to me," Laia said.

"He did look tired, but he always looks tired when he's excited. He used to stay up all night examining his books and checking his facts before finally going down to the excavation and discovering something wonderful—at least that's what he did in Greece." Rose shrugged her shoulders.

"But what could he find at Pemberton?" Thalia asked.

"I have no idea. I supposed we'll find out when he returns."

St. John followed the butler into the Graces' drawing room.

It only took one look at Miss Grace for him to know that Georgiana had been right. She was not only beautiful and intelligent, but just being in her presence made him happy. It had been so long since he had felt this way about a woman, he hadn't even recognized his love for her when it had been directly in front of him.

He had spent most of the night thinking about what Georgiana had said, and he had figured it out. He knew now what he must do.

Just as he had put St. John aside so many years ago, now he had to take him up again. He wanted—no, needed—to recapture that exuberance for life, that passion for learning, that drive for... well, everything that he'd had as a young man. He wanted to be *himself* once more.

And it would all begin with Rose.

"Mr. Fotheringay–Phipps, Miss Grace," the butler intoned. "I shall inform Lady Farmington that you have a guest."

"If you don't mind, Miss Grace, I would prefer it if we could have some privacy," St. John said quickly.

The butler looked to his mistress for direction. She looked a little surprised at this, but then nodded. "An excellent idea. Do not worry, Reynolds, we shall leave the door open, and my sisters are nearby if I need any assistance."

The butler gave St. John a warning look before bowing himself out of the room.

St. John moved forward and handed Rose the bouquet of roses he had brought.

"Although they're not nearly as lovely as you, I could not resist the temptation," he said.

Rose flushed prettily. "Thank you."

Rose sat down in a chair by the empty fireplace, and indicated for him to take the opposite chair. "It is so nice that you could come to visit, Fungy."

"I would be honored if you would call me St. John, Miss Grace. It is my given name," he said, sitting down.

"Oh!" Rose gave a little, embarrassed laugh. "Isn't it funny? I never thought of you having a Christian name since you've already got a nickname."

He couldn't help but smile. "St. John is my given name. An unfortunate name, but mine, nonetheless."

"It's no more unfortunate than Euphrosyne, I assure you."

St. John laughed. "No, suppose not. But Rose is a beautiful name, and fits you very well. Would you mind if I called you by your given name?"

"No. Not at all. I would be honored," she said, flushing again.

He wasn't exactly sure where one started a marriage proposal. Was he supposed to get down on one knee right away and tell her of his undying love?

No, that didn't seem right. He should ease into it perhaps.

"Last night, Rose, I enjoyed your company a great deal," he began, awkwardly.

"As did I enjoy yours."

"The waltz..."

"Yes! It was very..." Rose trailed off.

"Special," St. John finished for her.

"Indeed."

St. John felt as if his heart would burst with joy. She had felt it too. She had felt the magic, the love, that incredible moment they had had together. But how could she not? It was so strong, so tangible.

Vestiges of the desire he had felt for her after their dance still played throughout his body. To hold her in his arms, feel her sweet lips against his, and, oh, so much more! The thought was making him distinctly uncomfortable.

But she was saying something and he had missed the beginning of it.

"...such a good friend, er, St. John. I know that I can trust you."

"Of course!" he said quickly, as she paused for breath.

She smiled at him warmly. "Then, perhaps, since you are such a good friend, you wouldn't mind giving me a little advice? I have a small... dilemma."

St. John returned her smile. "You know that you can ask anything of me."

A Dandy In Disguise

"It is just..." she suddenly seemed very uncomfortable. Studying her hands in her lap, she said, "Last night... Lord Kirtland danced with me *three* times. I'm not certain, but I think that might mean something."

A tightness formed in St. John's throat.

"Three times, you say?"

"Yes."

St. John cleared his throat and tried to breathe.

"Well, er, how do you feel about him?" He hated asking the question, but he had to know.

"I like him very much." Rose seemed incapable of looking at him. This would have been a good sign if not for the words that continued to pour from her mouth. "And he's wealthy, which is..." she paused, flushing a little. "...important for my family just now. He's an archeologist as well, did you know that?" Finally her eyes met his.

"Er, yes, I think I might have heard something to the affect," he managed, trying to keep his face blank.

"I'm just not certain what I should do," she finished, once again unable to meet his eyes.

Twenty

"I'm afraid you're going to have to let me ruminate on it," St. John said.

After so many years of protecting himself, of avoiding all romantic situations, of making sure that no woman could ever come near to breaking his heart the way Georgiana had, he'd finally opened himself up.

And *this* is what he got.

St. John almost laughed at the irony. He almost cried, so acute was the pain.

He stood up and turned toward the door. He had to go. He had to leave before he unmanned himself. Before his shattered heart cut through the shell of his façade.

"Fungy? Are you all right?" Rose stood up as well. "I hope I haven't said anything..."

"What? No! No, of course not. I am sorry, Miss Grace, I just realized... there is an appointment I am late for." He paused. "Regarding Lord Kirtland—I would advise patience. He is an intelligent man. I am certain that he is merely waiting for the right opportunity to... to make his intentions clear. Good day, Miss Grace."

Without looking back, he strode from the room as quickly as he could. There was nothing else he could do.

Rose just stood there watching him leave.

Why had he done that?

Rose sat down on the sofa. She had stolen a peek at him through her lashes and had caught the brief look of hurt on his face—for a moment she had thought it must have been her imagination.

But it hadn't been. She should never have said anything about dancing with Lord Kirtland! She had even told her sisters she could not do such a thing, and then it had just slipped out of her mouth before she even realized it. She had been entirely too comfortable with Fungy.

Rose got up and began to pace back and forth, furiously kicking the hem of her dress in front of her as her stride lengthened.

She had upset Fungy, terribly.

How could she have done this? How could she have hurt the man she cared for so much? Who, clearly, cared for her much more than she for him, although in a very different way. It was so clear to her now.

Fungy loved her.

And she had just told him that she was interested in marrying someone else!

Rose dropped back down onto the sofa once more.

He *must* be in love with her. Why else would he have looked at her in that way at the ball last night while they danced? Why else had he been so sweet and kind to her at the card party, and at the park—not to mention all of the other times he had rescued her or her sisters from their own folly?

And now, as thanks, she'd been unbearably cruel to him.

Tears began trickling down Rose's face, but she did nothing to stop them.

How could she have done this!

She felt the warmth of another hand grasp onto hers. Raising her eyes, she saw that Laia had sat next to her on the sofa. She was joined a moment later by Thalia.

"What has happened?"

"Rose, are you all right?" the two girls said in unison.

Rose rested her head against Laia's shoulder, but said nothing. Her throat was still too constricted with shame to be able to say anything just yet.

Laia soothed her hair while Thalia took Rose's other hand and held it comfortingly.

"Was it Fungy?" Laia asked. "Was he mean to you? What did he say?"

"Did you ask him about Lord Kirtland?"

"Did he say it was hopeless?"

Rose sniffed and sat up again wiping away the tears from her cheeks. She swallowed around the lump in her throat. "He was not mean to me. It was I who was cruel beyond words to him."

"What do you mean? What happened?"

Rose told her sisters exactly what had occurred, from the moment Fungy had walked into the room, to the time when he'd left it so abruptly.

They were silent for a few minutes after, digesting what she had told them.

"So you think that he loves you?" Thalia finally asked, quietly.

"Of course he does! Weren't you listening?" Laia asked her little sister scornfully.

"Please, Laia, do not be hurtful," Rose said, laying a hand gently on Laia's knee. "Yes, Thalia, I believe that he does—and that I have hurt him a great deal by telling him about Lord Kirtland's interest in me and that I... Whatever must he think of me?"

"But it wasn't your fault," Thalia objected.

"You didn't ask him outright how to bring Lord Kirtland up to scratch, you simply told him what anyone else at the ball would have seen if they'd been paying attention," Laia added.

Rose shook her head sadly. "But I shouldn't have said anything."

The girls were silent once more, until Laia asked, "What are you going to do, Rose?"

Rose hung her head. "I don't know."

Her head had begun pounding as she'd told her tale to her sisters. Now, it was becoming increasingly unbearable.

"I think I will lie down for a bit. I have the most awful migraine. Later, I'll figure out what to do." Rose got up slowly and walked to her room. For once, her sisters didn't try to follow.

※

As the three sisters sat subdued at breakfast the following morning, Reynolds entered the dining room with a note for Rose.

"What is it, Rose?" Aunt Farmington asked, as soon as she had broken open the seal.

"Who is it from?" Thalia said, around a mouthful of egg.

Rose wiped at the tears that began to slide down her cheeks as she read the note.

Laia snatched it from her limp hand and read out loud.

Dear Miss Grace,

Thinking over your dilemma, I have come to the conclusion that what is needed is an Opportunity. Therefore, I will be hosting a small party at Kensington Gardens this coming Friday. No word of the purpose of the gathering will be told to anyone. It will simply be an afternoon of pleasure for a few close friends of mine.

I do hope that this date is convenient for you.

Sincerely,

Your good friend,

St. John Fotheringay–Phipps

"What is the purpose of the party?" Aunt Farmington asked. "What dilemma do you have, my dear?"

Rose wiped her eyes with her napkin. "How to get Lord Kirtland to propose to me," she said quietly.

Aunt Farmington's eyes widened.

After being brought up to date on what had happened, Aunt Farmington shook her head. "You told a gentleman that you were expecting a proposal from someone else?"

"I didn't tell him that, precisely. And I didn't realize at the time that Fungy was in love with me!" Rose protested.

"I am extremely disappointed in you, Rose. The nerve... how could you?" She paused in her horror to pick up Fungy's note and reread it. "Well, you have no choice but to attend this little gathering of Fungy's, since he is holding it for you."

"Yes. I shall reply to him immediately."

"And you shall thank him most sincerely!" Aunt Farmington said sternly.

"Yes, ma'am. No need to remind me of that."

"I have never heard of such cheek! And to get away with it, by all that is..."

"Please, Aunt Farmington, please don't make this any worse," Rose pleaded.

"I assure you Rose knows that what she did was wrong, ma'am, she has been berating herself for it since yesterday," Laia added, trying to be helpful.

Aunt Farmington just frowned at all three girls.

"St. John, this was a wonderful idea," Georgiana said, taking a sip of her wine. She was looking, if possible, even more lovely than she had at the ball. Her rich rust-colored walking dress brought out the warmth in her eyes. She was wearing a very fetching bonnet to match. She looked completely relaxed on the blanket that had been laid on the soft grass for her and the other ladies. St. John had found the perfect spot for their picnic.

Kew Gardens was lovely at this time of year. The grass was lush, the trees provided shade and there were paths through the gardens and even a few spots where a tête—à—tête could be had.

"Oh, indeed, Fungy. My goodness, I can't believe how long it's been since we were all together like this," Teresa, Merry's wife, said. She was sitting near Georgiana, and held a parasol so as to protect her fair skin from the harmful rays of the sun.

St. John stood up. "Well, then, a toast. To old friends," he raised his glass toward Georgiana, as well as to Merry, Sin, Julian and their wives, "and to new." He raised his glass toward Rose and Lord Kirtland.

"Hear, hear!"

"To friends!"

"Well, I, for one, think that Fungy invited us all here just so that we could admire his new way of tying his neckcloth!" Cassandra, Lady Huntley, said with a touch of laughter in her voice.

"Yes, Fungy, what do you call that style?" Julian asked, absently tugging at one his wife's blond curls which had escaped from the knot on top of her head. They made a striking pair, her fair English loveliness a perfect contrast to his dark-skinned good looks.

St. John gave a little bow, pleased that his friends had noticed this exceptional new way of tying his neckcloth that he had created just that morning. "Call it the Friendship knot—in honor of the occasion, of course."

"It looks unusually simple. Did it take you hours to achieve?" Sin's wife, Sara, asked, leaning forward her diminutive frame so that she could get a better look.

"But, of course," St. John answered, with mock surprise.

"What a question! Fungy always takes hours over his neckcloth," Merry said, laughing.

"*Au contraire*, my esteemed cousin," St. John began.

"No, I was quite impressed. It only took him twenty minutes that last time I was present at the event," Julian interrupted.

"Only twenty minutes?" Sin asked, disbelievingly, but with a laugh in his voice.

"Why don't you spend so much time on your neckcloth, Sin? Maybe then you could look bang up to the mark like Fungy," his wife laughed.

"What a waste of time," Lord Kirtland said quietly.

"Ah, but not if you care to make a good impression on the ladies, Lord Kirtland," Georgiana said, turning around to look at him. "I'm just surprised that my dear old friend St. John, who could barely be bothered to button his waistcoat when I last saw him, would now spend the time necessary to make such an impression."

"Always dressed properly!" St. John protested.

"Perhaps, but only just barely so," she grudgingly admitted to the guffaws of St. John's friends.

"I can't imagine Fungy not dressed to perfection," Rose said.

"No, nor can I," Sara agreed.

"He's always been impeccably attired since I've known him," Teresa added.

"You ladies didn't know me in my salad days, that's all," St. John said.

"I remember those days," Merry said.

"I prefer to forget them," Sin retorted, to much laughter.

"Well, it's a lovely day," St. John said, stepping toward the ladies. "I am going take the beautiful Lady Mirthwood for a walk, if she would so honor me?" He held out his hand to help Georgiana up.

Before offering his arm to Georgiana, St. John watched out of the corner of his eye as Rose took Lord Kirtland's proffered arm.

It killed him to think that he would be the one responsible for enabling the woman he loved to marry another. And yet, what could he do? If she loved Kirtland, there was nothing St. John could do to make her love him instead.

On the other hand, if Kirtland didn't take advantage of this golden opportunity that St. John had just dropped into his lap, then it would clearly show that he wasn't worthy of her affections. And in that case, there would be nothing stopping St. John from doing all that he could to secure Rose's affection. If Kirtland didn't propose today, he would be a bigger fool than St. John could believe possible.

"Do you wish to follow them, St. John?"

"What?"

"I think you are going to strain your neck if you continue to watch Miss Grace walk in that direction, while we are walking this way. However, if you wish, we could follow them."

St. John felt his face heat with embarrassment. He had not meant to be so obvious, and he had not meant to ignore Georgiana either. "No, not at all. Please forgive me. I was merely distracted for a moment. Although how I could be so, when *I* have the most beautiful and fascinating woman present with me, I honestly don't know."

"Ah yes, that is why I put up with you so long ago—you are the most atrociously wonderful flirt I have ever had the privilege to know!"

St. John laughed and gave Georgiana a magnificent leg. "Too kind, Georgiana, as always, you are too kind."

Twenty-One

"I'm happy you're feeling better," Lord Kirtland said, as they strolled slowly across the grass. "I was quite worried when I received your note Tuesday afternoon saying that you were too ill to attend the card party."

"Thank you. It was just a temporary ailment," Rose said, trying to remain calm. Ever since Fungy had stood up and announced that he was going to take Lady Mirthwood for a walk, Rose felt as if her heart had been lodged in her throat.

This was it. This was the opportunity for Lord Kirtland to get her alone and to propose.

"It's a shame it kept you from the party. Aiken won a monkey from George Cole. It was quite exciting to watch. Cole is very good, you know."

"Oh yes? I am sorry to have missed it," Rose said. If things worked out as she hoped this afternoon, she need never attend another card party again.

"I was looking forward to giving you the opportunity to win back the money you owe me from last week's party."

"That is kind of you," Rose said, although it was not particularly kind to remind her of her debt. Rose shook her head to herself. She would think nothing but good thoughts of Lord Kirtland today. Today was a special day.

He was going to propose. She knew he would. It was what had kept her stomach feeling like it was tied up in knots all day. She hadn't been able to eat a bite of the beautiful display of food Fungy had provided them. If all went right, she would soon be engaged to this man. Rose took a deep, calming breath and gave Lord Kirtland a little smile.

What if he didn't propose? Rose almost stopped walking as the horrible thought echoed in her mind. She forced herself to continue on, however, as if nothing was wrong. But what would she do? All of Fungy's hard work would be for nothing, her family would be ruined, she would need to find another gentleman to marry quickly—she might even be forced to marry someone old and smelly. Rose nearly shuddered at the thought.

And following this dreadful thought was one that scared her even more—what would she do if he *did* propose?

It was what she wanted, she knew that. But it didn't make her any less scared. She was in love with Lord Kirtland, she reminded herself. And he was the key to her family's future, thanks to his wealth.

No, it was going to be fine. Absolutely fine. They would have a wonderful life together excavating archaeological ruins. They would be a team, just like her own parents had been. Her sisters would get introduced to society properly and would both be able to wait to marry until they had fallen completely, head–over–heels in love.

Still, Rose's stomach refused to relax.

They came to a large folly, which provided a very nice respite from the heat of the day. Although Rose had remembered to bring her parasol, she was still quite warm. That, combined with her nerves, made her feel a bit uncomfortable, but the folly was lovely and cool.

A Dandy In Disguise

Sitting down on the cold stone bench, Rose looked out at the broad green lawns. They stretched on for what looked like nearly a mile before they dropped down to a very pretty ornamental lake.

Sitting sideways on the bench facing the lake, she didn't see Lord Kirtland sit down behind her. But she was very much aware of him. Just knowing that he was sitting so very close to her sent shivers down her spine.

She held tightly onto the handle of her parasol, hoping that Lord Kirtland wouldn't notice her shaking fingers.

"Miss Grace," Lord Kirtland placed his hand on top of hers. "Perhaps I presume too much, but may I say that I find you an extremely attractive young lady?"

Rose turned around and looked into Lord Kirtland's dark eyes. He was looking very serious and not a little forbidding, his eyebrows drawn down over his deep-set brown eyes.

She swallowed hard. He was probably as nervous as she was, she thought.

"Thank you, my lord," Rose managed to say.

"I find you attractive not only in your physical beauty, but in the beauty of your mind as well. And as we both have a great love of archeology, I believe that we would suit uncommonly well."

"I completely agree!" Rose blurted out.

Lord Kirtland laughed, and seemed to relax a little. "Just think of the archaeological expeditions we could embark on together if we married. With your father's connections and no financial worries, we could go to Egypt and join in the work exploring more of the fabulous tombs there—perhaps finding more gold jewelry and priceless sarcophagi."

"I did love Egypt. The tombs are filled with such fascinating hieroglyphs and paintings," Rose agreed.

"May I speak with your father, then?"

"Oh, yes, my lord, as soon as he returns from the country," Rose breathed as she watched Lord Kirtland's face come closer to her own.

This time she did not flinch or turn away, but forced herself not to move while he gently pressed his lips to hers.

It was an odd sensation, his lips and breath hot against her face. There were none of the tingles she had expected, but rather a chill that brought goose bumps to her arms. Rose didn't understand it, but she supposed that this is what it felt like when one was in love.

She tried to kiss him back, but didn't want to seem too bold. And honestly, she was not entirely sure what to do.

Finally, he moved back. She gave him a nervous little smile, and then looked down at her hands still clutching her parasol. Hopefully, he was happy with her attempt, but she was really too nervous to even look at his face to see.

But it was over. It was done! He had proposed and she had accepted. He now only needed to make the arrangements with her father and everything would be settled.

The relief was overwhelming. All of a sudden, Rose felt like she could breathe again, and she had the overwhelming urge to throw her arms around Lord Kirtland's neck and laugh for the sheer joy of knowing that everything was going to be all right now.

Everything was going to be absolutely perfect! Rose nearly giggled.

A Dandy In Disguise

Lord Kirtland would forgive her gaming debts, he would pay their bills, and she would have the money she would need to see her sisters launched into society properly.

Hopefully, she would be able to return to England for Laia's coming out. Although being on an archaeological dig again would be wonderful, and she was truly looking forward to going back to Egypt.

She caught Lord Kirtland's eye. He gave her a questioning little smile. "I am very glad that you are happy about this."

A giggle finally did escape from her mouth. "Yes, my lord, I am very happy. You are too, I hope?" Rose asked quickly.

"Yes, my dear. Very happy," he said. And indeed, he did look happy—although relieved, perhaps, would have been a more accurate description for the expression on his face. Rose supposed that he had been just as nervous as she was. But now everything was just as it ought to be.

If only Rose didn't have this feeling of unease in the pit of her stomach. Well, she was sure that it would go away as she got to know Lord Kirtland better.

Twenty-Two

"Oh, what a lovely aspect." Lady Mirthwood's voice was saying rather loudly as she and Fungy stepped into the folly. "I have so missed English gardens. You know they try to copy them in America, but somehow, they just aren't the same."

Lord Kirtland immediately stood up and moved away from Rose, as if they had been caught kissing.

Rose supposed they had, but she was grateful for the interruption and the company. She was not entirely sure how much she liked Lady Mirthwood—she was entirely too familiar with Fungy—but right now she would have welcomed almost anyone. And she did so want to share the news with Fungy. His plan had worked to perfection, just as she had known it would.

"Lord Kirtland, Miss Grace. Didn't see you here. Please excuse us for interrupting," Fungy said, stopping just inside the folly.

"It is no problem. None at all. We... ah, well, you may be the first to congratulate us. Miss Grace has just consented to become my wife."

Rose stood up, looking at Fungy perhaps closer than was polite. Did he seem upset? Yes, she decided, he most certainly did, but just for a fleeting moment. Now he was hiding it manfully.

Rose bit the inside of her lip. She didn't wish to say anything that might further his hurt, but she did so desperately want to thank him.

"Congratulations," Lady Mirthwood said, pulling Rose's attention away from Fungy. She gave Rose a little smile that didn't quite reach her eyes. Somehow, she didn't seem as happy as Rose would have expected.

Did Lady Mirthwood know of Fungy's infatuation with her? Was that why her reaction was so subdued? She must. But then, why wasn't she happy? She could have Fungy all to herself now—and from the way she behaved with him, in such an obviously intimate way, Rose imagined that that was just what she would want.

Rose wasn't jealous, she reassured herself. She just wished Lady Mirthwood would not be so conspicuous.

Fungy tried for a little more animation in his response to the news . As if abruptly coming to life, he said, "Excellent! Lucky man."

He reached out and took Lord Kirtland's hand, pumping it up and down. "So happy for you, Miss Grace." He then took Rose's hand and simply pressed it meaningfully between both of his, looking deeply into her eyes.

The heat from his hand shot up her arm and sent tingles running through Rose's veins, immediately dispelling her chills of a few moments ago.

Rose gave him her most grateful smile, trying to convey her thanks to him for what he had done, her recognition of her deep debt to him. His smile softened and he gave her a little nod. He understood, as she had been certain he would.

Georgiana was unusually quiet on the way home after the picnic. St. John didn't mind. He had enough to think about himself.

He had to admit that he had been disappointed, if not at all surprised, that Kirtland had come through.

He'd hoped the man wouldn't come up to scratch, but now that he thought about it, he knew it'd been an unreasonable hope. If he had been in Kirtland's place, he would have jumped at the opportunity to propose to Rose without a moment's hesitation—just as Kirtland had.

No, Kirtland was no fool, of that he was certain.

Georgiana's warm hand on his own startled St. John from his thoughts. She gave him a consoling smile.

She knew. Naturally, she'd known right away that he'd been in love with Rose, even before he had realized it himself. And now she knew just how upset he was that Rose had become engaged to another. She knew him so well. Better than he knew himself, at times.

He pulled up to her town house and then jumped down to help her descend from his phaeton.

"Would you mind if I stepped inside with you for a moment?" he asked, suddenly knowing exactly what he must do.

She smiled up at him. "I would like that."

As they entered the neat little house, Georgiana instructed her footman to take care of St. John's equipage for a short time. St. John gave him a nod, and then followed Georgiana up to her drawing room.

She immediately poured him out a glass of brandy and then took some wine for herself, sitting down on a pink scroll–back sofa. He took a fortifying sip and a deep breath, and set the glass aside.

Instead of taking the seat she offered to him, he knelt at her feet and took her free hand in his own. "Georgiana, I would be most honored if you would marry me."

The room was immediately filled with the beautiful sound of Georgiana's laughter. That is, until she looked into his eyes and saw that he was utterly serious.

"Oh, St. John." She ran her hand along his cheek in a motherly fashion. "I know that you are upset over Miss Grace, but truly, this is not the answer."

"I am not doing this because of Miss Grace," St. John said, standing up again. "I have been thinking of this ever since we met at the ball the other night," he lied.

It would not do to let Georgiana know she'd hit the nail right on the head. And what were a few little lies, when it ensured that he would not die alone and unloved by anyone?

"I simply do not believe I could stand by and watch you marry someone else again. You are too beautiful and too special a woman to live as a widow for very long. I know that if I do not ask you now, it will be too late and I will have missed what may have been my last opportunity to have you for my very own."

Georgiana stood up. Putting down her own drink, she put her arms around St. John's neck and kissed him deeply.

He tasted the wine on her tongue and the sweetness of her mouth. That, coupled with the feel of her luscious body pressed against his, should have sent shivers of excitement through him.

But it didn't. He felt nothing—nothing but the remnants of what used to be his great love for this woman, now a great platonic love and friendship.

Was it enough to last him the rest of his life? He supposed it had to be. It was the only choice he had. He deepened his kiss, but felt her pull away.

"My dearest St. John," she smiled up at him. "You know that I cannot marry a man who is in love with someone else—not even if that man is you."

"But..."

Georgiana pressed her finger to his lips. "No. You cannot deny it, my dear. I am sorry she has engaged herself to marry Lord Kirtland. Not just for your sake, even."

St. John stopped as he was about to reach down to pick up his glass of brandy. "What do you mean?" he said, straightening up again.

Georgiana gave a little shrug. "I'm not entirely sure, but there is something about Lord Kirtland. I don't know if it's because he's wrong for Miss Grace, or if it's something about him personally, but something about their engagement just rubs me the wrong way."

St. John sat down with his drink. "No, you're right. It's Kirtland, I'm sure of it. I've had bad feelings ever since I met him. At first I just thought it was jealousy, but I'm beginning to think otherwise."

"Well, whatever it is, I just hope Miss Grace realizes it before it's too late for her."

This worried St. John more than he could say, and it seemed that Georgiana felt the same way.

His dear, sweet Rose could get trapped into marriage with this fellow for the rest of her life—it was a terrifying thought.

༄

"Well done! That is excellent news," Aunt Farmington exclaimed "Girls, why do you not congratulate your sister? You should be very happy for her."

"Congratulations, Rose," Laia said with almost no emotion whatsoever to her voice.

Thalia showed only a little more emotion—she frowned."I am very happy for you, Rose."

"My, what excitement and joy!" Rose said, feeling like a balloon that had burst. Deflated, she dropped down on the sofa. "I thought that you would both be happy for me."

"We are!" Laia exclaimed, finally moving over and giving her sister a hug. "We just hope that you are doing the right thing. Marrying the right man."

"We truly want you to be happy, Rose," Thalia said coming over and sitting at her sister's feet.

Rose gave her sisters' hands a squeeze. "I know you do, and I *will* be happy. Lord Kirtland is definitely the right man for me. He is everything I could possibly want in a husband. I've explained this to you before."

"Yes, it's just..."

"I know what it is," Rose interrupted her sister. "You simply don't know Lord Kirtland. I'm certain that if you got to know him better, you would be just as thrilled as I am."

She jumped up and strode over to the escritoire. Pulling out a sheet of paper, she said, "I shall write him a note asking him to come and meet you both. I just know that after you've met him, you'll like him and be happy for us."

Twenty-Three

A ride in the park wasn't exactly what Rose had had in mind for her sisters' first meeting with Lord Kirtland. But she was happy that her sisters would be able to spend a little time with her new fiancé, even if in a public setting.

"Oh, look, Rose, there is that duke we saw the last time," Laia said, trying to nudge her horse forward so that she could ride next to her sister.

"Yes—Lord Hawksmore," Rose said, giving a delicate nod of her head towards him. "But Laia, please do rein in. It wouldn't be right for you to abandon Thalia, and there isn't room for the four of us to ride abreast."

Laia gave a little pout and then fell behind again to ride next to her sister.

Rose turned and gave Lord Kirtland a smile. "I am sorry, my lord, I didn't mean to push you aside."

"Quite all right. Hopefully, your sister will remember her manners this time and stay where she belongs."

Rose took a quick look at Lord Kirtland. Had he really meant the comment to sound so unkind? He had a bit of a smile on his face, however, so Rose assumed he had made a joke. She forced out a little giggle in response.

A Dandy In Disguise

She looked around at the fashionable men and women of the *haute ton* who were riding through the park. Did they know? Did they know that she and Lord Kirtland were engaged? It was probably much too soon for anyone to have learned about it, but deep in her heart she wished they had. She wanted everyone to know. She wanted to shout it out to the world.

She was also quite desperate for her sisters to make a good impression on Lord Kirtland, and vice–versa. But so far, that had proved impossible with the way they were riding. Perhaps she could figure out a way for her to switch places with Laia, and then with Thalia, so that her sisters could at least speak with him.

"Do you think, Miss Grace, that you might be interested in viewing a private collection of antiquities?" Lord Kirtland asked, pulling her attention back to himself.

"I would indeed," Rose answered, without hesitation.

"Excellent. I have recently had the honor of meeting Sir John Soane, and he invited me to view what he calls his 'Academy of Architecture'. I believe he has some very fine pieces from both Egypt and Greece on display."

"That sounds..."

"Oh, Rose, look, there is Fungy!" Thalia called out.

Rose turned around in her saddle. "Please, Thalia! Lower your voice. I am very happy you have spotted our friend, but you must not shout so loud that everyone in the vicinity is aware of it as well," she said, with much more severity than she had intended. She never had actually given her sisters that lesson in deportment she'd said she would, and now she was regretting it.

She turned back and stole a look at Lord Kirtland to see how he had reacted, and was a little disturbed to see that he was looking approvingly at her. She gave him a small smile and asked, "Would you mind, sir, if we stopped for a moment to speak with him?"

"No, not at all."

It turned out that she need not have asked, for the gentleman himself had spotted them and was riding over to greet them. He was accompanied by Lady Mirthwood, riding a dappled gray mare.

Were the two of them inseparable? Rose's thought was accompanied by a flash of anger. She immediately quelled the feeling, reprimanding herself sternly, while giving them both her brightest smile.

Fungy, dressed impeccably as always, was mounted on a fine black gelding with a white blaze on his nose. "Oh, Fungy, what an exceedingly fine horse," Thalia exclaimed as he got closer.

Fungy gave a little bow from the saddle. "Why, thank you, Miss Thalia. I have heard that you were a very fine judge of horseflesh."

The girl beamed happily.

"How do you do, Lady Mirthwood? It is good to see you again," Rose said, doing her best to be polite and kind. If Fungy was close to the woman, then the very least Rose could do was to be courteous.

"You are looking very well today, Miss Grace. You have a very becoming blush to your cheeks," Lady Mirthwood said.

"Oh!" Rose put a hand to her cheeks, but couldn't imagine why they were flushed. Perhaps her happiness with the day? Or with her engagement? Her happiness in seeing Fungy again—and Lady Mirthwood, of course, she added. Why, it could be so many different reasons.

"It is probably the heat, that is all," she said, laughing off her sudden embarrassment.

A Dandy In Disguise

Rose was thrilled when Fungy managed to position his horse between her and Lord Kirtland, for she particularly wanted a private word with him.

She leaned forward in order to speak more softly to him while Lady Mirthwood and Lord Kirtland exchanged pleasantries.

"Fungy, I just cannot thank you enough for what you did yesterday. I really do not deserve such a good friend as you have shown yourself to be."

"Just seeing you happy is all the thanks that I need. And what happened to you calling me by my given name?" he teased.

He spoke just as quietly as she had, but somehow he made it seem so intimate and exciting. His deep, rich voice sent tingles through Rose, warming her in odd places.

She gave an embarrassed laugh. "I do apologize. You have been so good to me, St. John. Indeed, I do feel that we are close enough friends now so that I may address you by your given name. I promise to do so from now on."

"Miss Grace, your sisters are an abomination!" Lord Kirtland's voice interrupted, dispelling all of her good feelings.

"I beg your pardon?" she said, straightening her back as she turned to him. She desperately hoped that she had misheard him.

"Just look at them, galloping off like... like hoydens. It is beyond words how rude and inappropriate their behavior is—in the park, at the height of the promenade!"

Her heart leapt into her throat. She hadn't even heard them move off she'd been so focused on St. John. She turned back to him, but he had already turned his horse around and was about to set off after her wayward sisters. "Have no fear, Rose, I will see that they come to no harm, nor accidentally cause any."

Immediately she felt relieved, knowing that he would take care of everything. "Thank you, St. John. I knew I could count on you," she said quickly, as he thundered off.

Still, she could not help but be worried. The park was so crowded today that the galloping of Thalia and Laia's horses through the crowded bridle paths was sure to startle a number of other horses, if not worse. She sincerely hoped that no one would be injured.

"My goodness, are your sisters always so daring?" Lady Mirthwood asked.

"Daring is not the word I would use, my lady. Disobedient would be my guess. Either that, or so poorly raised that they know no better," Lord Kirtland said angrily. "And after their behavior so far today, I would assume the latter."

Rose opened her mouth to protest his harsh words, but worried about making a scene in public herself.

But just as quickly as this thought entered Rose's mind, she threw it right back out again. This was no time to be timid and ladylike. These were her sisters he had just insulted!

"How dare you, Lord Kirtland!" she said as quietly as she could while trying not to make too much of a scene in public. "My sisters and I may have been raised in an unconventional manner, but that is only to be expected in a foreign country and on an expedition. My parents did the best they could under the circumstance, and I think they did an exceptional job." She paused for breath, her horse shifting under her, feeling her anger." If Laia and Thalia do not always behave just as they should, then perhaps it is my fault for being too lenient with them. I am the one who has been in charge of them since my mother's death over a year ago, and indeed for much of their lives."

"A child bringing up other children? No wonder they are so ignorant," Lord Kirtland shook his head sadly.

"I am no child, sir," Rose replied furious at his condescension.

"Miss Laia and Thalia *are* still children, my lord. You must remember that, and not be so harsh on them," Lady Mirthwood said, coming to Rose's aid.

Lord Kirtland raised his eyebrows and turned back to Rose. "How old are your sisters, Miss Grace?"

"Thalia is fifteen and Laia seventeen."

He gave Lady Mirthwood a smug look. "They are not children, Lady Mirthwood. They are old enough to know better." Rose could not respond due to the return of St. John with the two girls.

"Oh, St. John, I cannot thank you enough! Girls, what have you to say for yourselves?" Rose said, spurring her horse forward to look severely at her sisters.

They were both looking very flushed as well as a little repentant, but both still had that twinkle of mischief in their eyes.

"We have already had a word," St. John said.

"Well, I think that they deserve more than just a word! A good beating would be more like..." Lord Kirtland began.

"My lord! Thank you very much, but I will deal with my sisters as I see fit," Rose said, sternly.

"Oh, no! They were just having a bit of a lark," St. John said, giving them a wink. "No harm done—to them or to anyone else. And I'm certain they won't do it again. Will you, ladies?"

The two girls covered up their giggles, but shook their heads.

Rose gave them a little smile, and to St. John as well. He had clearly done an excellent job in informing them of their mistake in such a way that they would neither repeat it, nor feel so rebellious that they would go out and cause more trouble. Firm but gentle—that was the way to deal with Laia and Thalia, as Rose knew.

"I believe it is time we headed for home, my lord," Rose said to Lord Kirtland.

"Indeed, perhaps well past."

She turned back to St. John and Lady Mirthwood. "I am so sorry for the trouble we've caused. It was wonderful to see you again."

The two waved them off amiably.

Lord Kirtland led Rose and her sisters out the nearest gate and then back towards their home.

As they trotted sedately down the lane, Rose felt that she should try and make amends with her fiancé. Perhaps he would understand if she just explained the situation to him.

"My lord, you must not be so angry with the girls," she tried. "They were clearly itching for a little fun after having to ride so sedately around the park with little amusement," she said.

Lord Kirtland turned to her, his face still a little pinched with annoyance. "Miss Grace, girls the ages of your sisters should know to behave better. Indeed, they should count themselves lucky to have so *much* as a sedate walk in the park, especially at the height of the promenade." To Rose's dismay, he became implacable. "No, when they are under my control, such behavior will not only not be tolerated, but punished appropriately."

Rose quickly turned to look behind her at her sisters, giving them a silent, imploring look to not speak a word of what she was sure they were thinking. Fortunately, they understood, and kept quiet until they had said good–bye to Lord Kirtland and seen their horses taken away to the stable.

But once inside their own drawing room, they let loose.

"Rose, how *could* you not defend us?"

"He is the most *horrendous* man I ever hope to meet!"

"You cannot mean to actually marry him!"

"Oh no, Rose, you cannot. Papa could not force you to do so, could he?"

Rose held up her hands to stem the flow of their words.

"I *did* defend you, Laia! I did so quite strongly while St. John—er, Fungy was off rescuing you from your own folly. Even Lady Mirthwood put in a word in your defense. But I must say that what you did was truly indefensible. You know that running off pell–mell like that could have hurt someone or yourselves."

She stopped to take a breath and shake her head reprovingly. But unbidden, a smile forced its way onto her lips. Before she could quash it, a giggle burst out, which she quickly hid behind her hand.

But it was no use. Before she knew it, she was working hard to contain her laughter.

Her sisters joined her immediately, and soon the three girls were laughing hysterically.

When Rose finally caught her breath, she said, "It was really too bad of you. But goodness, I cannot blame you at all. A more staid and boring outing and with so little to amuse yourselves... Even I was itching for a good gallop!"

"Oh, Rose," Thalia jumped up and threw her arms around her sister's neck. "I am so happy that you are still you!"

"Whatever do you mean?"

"It is just that I thought you would become stiff and stuffy like Lord Kirtland now that you are engaged to him."

"Really, Rose, you cannot marry that man. He is awful!"

Rose bit her lip. Her sisters were right. How could she marry a man who had absolutely no sense of humor at all? Stiff and stuffy described him perfectly.

But did she really have a choice?

An ache forming in her chest, she shook her head. "I *have* to marry him. He's rich, and will solve all of our financial problems. He'll pay our debts, and next year I'll be able to sponsor Laia for her come-out. I really don't have an option."

The sad looks on her sisters' faces said it all. And it was just how she felt as well, now that she was beginning to know Lord Kirtland better.

There was one truth that this day's outing had taught her—Lord Kirtland was certainly not going to be the knight in shining armor she'd always fantasized about as a child.

"Don't worry. He's really not *that* bad. And remember, he is an archaeologist," she told her sisters, trying to shed some positive light on what was looking more and more like a dreadful mistake.

Twenty-Four

By the following Monday, when Lord Kirtland picked up Rose to take her to Sir John Soane's Academy of Architecture, enough time had passed so that she could distance herself from the events of that fateful ride in the park, and look at what had occurred rationally. She still did not blame her sisters for their behavior, but she was no longer quite so upset by Lord Kirtland's reaction.

The still outstanding bills, however, were strongly weighing on her mind. She had received notes once again from both the mantua maker and cloth merchant, reminding her of the money she owed. To make things worse, she still could not rid her mind of the debt she owed to Lord Kirtland himself.

There had to be something she could do to dispel these debts. And she wasn't sure that she could wait six months or a year until she was wed to do so.

No, she decided, it was time to come clean to Lord Kirtland. She couldn't tell him about the bills just yet, but perhaps she could speak to him about her gambling debts.

Surely he would forgive her the money she owed to him now that they were engaged to be married? Without a doubt, she had to ask. And as soon as possible, so that she could properly concentrate on Sir John's magnificent collection.

At the first opportunity, she broached the subject as delicately as she could. "My lord, there is a favor I was wondering if I might ask of you."

Lord Kirtland looked from a striking collection of Greek vases to her with a look of mild surprise. "What might that be?"

"It is concerning the vowel you wrote for me, to Mr. Aiken," she began.

"Oh? I will be happy to escort you to Lady Kemble's card party tomorrow night, so that you can try once again to win the money back," he offered.

"Thank you, but I was wondering, actually, if you might forgive the debt altogether?"

Lord Kirtland turned toward Rose rather swiftly, to her surprise. "What do you mean? I paid your debt for you, and now you want me to just forget it?"

"Well..." Rose swallowed hard.

"Miss Grace, are you suggesting that you wish to go back on your word?" Lord Kirtland asked, drawing down his eyebrows in a vicious way.

"I..."

"I paid your debt for you because I thought that you were honest. I trusted you." He turned around to fix his attention fully upon Rose. "That you would think so little of your own honor is appalling, Miss Grace."

"It is not that! I always do my utmost to hold to my word. In fact, I do not believe I have ever gone back on it," Rose said, horrified that he would think so little of her.

"Well, then, I trust that you *will* repay this debt."

"I... I cannot." The words came out as a whisper. She just could not say them outright.

Lord Kirtland froze at her words. An unpleasant little smile crept onto his face. "You surely do not mean that you cannot. You mean that you do not have the funds just at this moment. I understand, Miss Grace. Your father has been away and you have not yet received your pin money this quarter."

He turned and took a few steps away. With a nonchalant wave of his hand, he continued, "That is perfectly fine. I have no problems waiting until your father returns from his estate. You may pay me when it is convenient. And because we are engaged to be married, I shall not even charge you any interest on the loan."

Interest? Just the thought horrified her. She managed to squeak out a "But..."

"No. No need to thank me, Miss Grace. It is perfectly all right." He gave her another fleeting smile. "Of course, it is entirely possible that you shall win it all back tomorrow night and none of this will have been necessary at all."

He then turned away from her once again to move on to the exhibit in the next room. Rose followed him in silence. What was she going to do? There did not seem to be any way out, short of telling Lord Kirtland outright that neither she nor her father had the money to pay this debt. It didn't seem right to try and win it back either, especially since she no longer had any money with which to gamble.

She did the only thing her pricked pride would allow her.

"No. I thank you, my lord. I do not believe I shall be attending Lady Kemble's card party tomorrow night. I will find another way to pay you back, and as quickly as possible," Rose said finally. She turned back to the exhibit, but still could find no amusement in it.

It turned out to be a very bleak afternoon.

After reaching home, she explained all that had happened to her sisters. "But I just don't know what to do. I could not tell him that we don't have the money." She paused. "Papa will be incredibly angry when he finds out what I've done, and rightfully so."

Thalia and Laia just looked at each other. Clearly, they were at a loss as well. Thalia, always the optimist, said, "Don't worry, Rose, we'll figure *something* out."

"Yes, and after we do, you won't have to marry that horrid man after all," Laia added.

Rose smiled at her sisters, but could not imagine that they would be able to come up with anything either.

※

"Where is Laia?" Aunt Farmington asked the following evening, as she, Thalia, and Rose sat in the drawing room enjoying a quiet evening at home.

"She's gone to bed early. She wasn't feeling well," Thalia answered, hardly pausing in her practicing of the pianoforte.

"Really, I wasn't aware of this," Rose said, with real concern—Laia never got ill.

Thalia got a panicked look in her eye for a moment, but quickly focused her eyes downward to her fingers. "Oh yes, well, it's just a headache, I believe. I'm sure she'll be fine tomorrow."

"Well, that's a relief. I'm certain I wouldn't know what to do with a sick child," Aunt Farmington said.

Rose couldn't be fooled so easily, however. Not by either of her sisters. She slowly set aside her sewing. "I think I'll just take a peek in on her then, just to make sure everything is all right."

Thalia jumped up. "Oh, no, Rose, you needn't do that. I shall go up if you like."

Now she was certain that her sisters were up to something. "That's very kind of you, Thalia, but no, I'll go myself."

She walked quickly up to the room shared by her two younger sisters, Thalia following anxiously on her heels. As she expected, the room was empty. She went in anyway, and then turned on her youngest sister as soon as the door was closed.

"Where is she? And what are you two up to?"

Thalia was a little taken aback by the sudden attack. She recovered herself quickly, however. "She is just out doing what you refused to do," she said, crossing her arms defiantly.

"What do you mean?"

"I mean, she is out trying to win back the money you lost."

"But... but she doesn't even know how to play whist!"

"Yes, she does. We found a book at the lending library explaining exactly how to play. It even gave some tricks on how to win," Thalia said, quite thrilled with herself.

Rose opened her mouth, but simply could not put all of the thousands of thoughts and fears that were running through her mind into a coherent sentence.

How could her sister be so stupid as to put herself at risk with such an outrageous scheme? With what money was she playing? How did she get to the party? And what if someone recognized her?

On and on the questions went, increasing her worry with every passing moment until she tasted blood and realized she was biting her lip. There was only one thing to do, she realized with moan of chagrin—she had to go and save her!

Without a further word to her sister, she went straight to her own room and her armoire for her domino and mask. Of course, they were gone. Laia had taken them!

"Rose, what are you going to do?" Thalia asked. She had followed Rose into her room.

"I am going to fetch her, only..."

Rose began to pace. What was she to do? She could not go to a card party without some sort of mask to hide behind.

"Only what?"

"Laia took my domino and mask. I cannot go without them."

Then she remembered that she had an old cloak that had once belonged to her mother. It was quite tattered, but that hardly mattered just now. At least it had a large hood which she could use to hide herself. It would have to do.

It took Rose and Thalia a good ten or fifteen minutes to find it—wasted time that she did not have. The later she got to the card party, the later she could rescue Laia from the lure of the cards, and probably the more money they would owe.

"Make sure Aunt Farmington does not notice anything is amiss. I am counting on you," she whispered to her sister just before she slipped out the back door.

Twenty-Five

St. John drained the wine from his glass and then, without hesitation, filled it up again. There was something soothing in the wine, even though the alcohol had not yet begun to affect him. He would need another few glasses, he guessed, just to get him through another evening of appearing as if everything was normal.

Each day, it was becoming more and more difficult to assume his usual practiced ennui. He had actually been surprised at how easy it was to revert back to his old self—and how comfortable it had felt behaving that way.

But he could not do so tonight. Tonight, it was the normal Fungy who needed to make an appearance, and St. John would have to be suppressed once more.

With a sigh and another fortifying gulp, he turned to see the clothes his valet had carefully laid out for him to wear this evening.

"Thomas, what is this? How long have you been in my employ that you cannot put together a simple suit of clothes for me to wear?" he said. Now he had to deal with this, in addition to the pounding headache that had become his constant companion over the past few days? Something so simple, so utterly simple, and the man just could not manage it?

His valet looked down at the black pantaloons, which he had coupled with a dark green coat and a waistcoat with green and gold embroidery. "I beg your pardon, sir," he said, but then hesitated over which piece of the offending suit to remove.

Fungy gave him a minute to figure out what he had done wrong, but clearly the man was completely incapable. He snatched up the coat and tossed it at him. "Take out my black coat if you are having me wear black pantaloons, man."

"Yes, sir." Thomas hastened to do his master's bidding.

Immediately, St. John felt a stab of remorse shooting through him. He dropped back down into the chair in front of his dressing table, sighing and rubbing at his forehead. "I'm sorry, Thomas. Didn't mean to snap at you like that. Not your fault."

"If I may say so, sir, you have not been quite yourself the past few days," Thomas offered gently.

"No, I have not been sleeping well at all," St. John said, inspecting the reflection in his shaving mirror. The bags under his eyes had grown into pouches, and his usually sparkling eyes looked back at him rather dully.

Losing Rose to Kirtland had been more difficult than he could have imagined. Having Georgiana turn him down as well had completely destroyed any ideas he had had of marrying and starting a family.

Dreams of drowning still haunted his nights. And although he awoke each morning determined to live up to his own resolutions, with each day those resolutions seemed harder and harder to attain.

At least he still had Lord Halsbury and his assignment—although he didn't know how much closer he was to coming to a conclusion on that front either. Perhaps if he made a list of possible suspects...

St. John abandoned his valet and strode to the drawing room and his writing table, determined to at least have something tangible to show Lord Halsbury the next time they met.

Sitting down, he pulled out a piece of paper and pen, and opened his ink stand.

Who were the people he had watched so far? What had he to go on?

With his penknife, he slowly and carefully began sharpening his quill as he thought. *P.H., P.H.* —he could still think of only Lord Pemberton–Howe and Pip Haston among society members with those initials. He dipped his pen into the ink, and jotted down the first of the names on his paper.

Immediately, he crossed it off. It couldn't be Pemberton–Howe—he'd been out of town for the past week, and in that time Cole had lost nearly a thousand pounds. He also simply couldn't imagine Rose's rather unworldly father as the leader of a gambling scheme.

That left just Pip Haston. St. John was about to begin writing the name when he was interrupted by a knock on the door.

"Fungy! Still not dressed?" Julian said, strolling into the room.

"Ah, no. Sorry, just finishing something up."

Silently, he cursed his good friend for being so timely, and himself for having forgotten that he'd invited Julian to accompany him out.

He turned back to his paper, but felt Julian's presence right behind him. He was looking over his shoulder.

St. John could not let his friend know what he was up to—it would give rise to too many questions he didn't want to answer. Quickly, he switched to spelling out Haston's name phonetically in Greek, mentally thanking Rose for inspiring him to begin reading his classics again.

There was one other name he had meant to write... yes, Kirtland. He started to wrack his brain for the *k* sound in Greek, but then remembered that Kirtland was the man's title. What was his name? Ah, Roland Egerton. That was easy enough.

A thrill of excitement and remembrance of his youth sung through his veins as he wrote out the name phonetically in Greek. He still had it. He'd not completely forgotten everything—amazing how a language could come back so quickly after so many years.

Finally, he stood up and greeted Julian properly.

"Welcome, old man. Sorry about that," he said.

"Not a problem. Amazing how you can just write in, what is that, Greek? Just like that. Although, I suppose it's not too different from me being able to writing in Bengali. But still, your scribbles *are* all Greek to me," Julian said, laughing at his own joke.

St. John laughed too, determined to be merry, despite his earlier bout of moroseness. But when he turned back momentarily to the list he had made, he suddenly felt as if he had had the wind knocked out of him.

There it was, clearly written in his own neat hand, Roland Egerton in Greek — Ρολανδ Ηγηρτον.

P.H.

St. John staggered back a step.

"Fungy, are you all right?" Julian grabbed St. John's arm to support him.

St. John took a step forward to balance himself and turned to look Julian in the eye.

A Dandy In Disguise

"Of course! The man is an archeologist. What an idiot I am to not have thought of this. He certainly reads Greek, wouldn't be surprised if he even wrote in it occasionally. And signing a note... he wouldn't use his English initials..."

"What on earth are you talking about?" Julian asked, completely confused.

St. John laughed, relief overwhelming him, and gave Julian a hug. Running back to his room, he called over his shoulder, "I'm a genius, Julian! Just be happy to know that you are friends with an absolute genius!"

Julian laughed. "I always knew that, Fungy. I just wish I could sometimes follow what you were saying." Julian came into St. John's room as he was just finishing buttoning his pantaloons.

"No need, my friend." Now, St. John thought to himself as he tied his neckcloth, he only needed to catch that rascal Kirtland at his own game.

When his neckcloth was tied to perfection, he asked, "Where were we supposed to go this evening?"

"Lady Baskin's soiree."

"Ah, right. Mind if we go to Lady Kemble's card party instead?"

"Not terribly. Is there a reason why you would rather go there?"

"Yes. Isn't it obvious?" St. John laughed.

"Fungy," Julian put his hand on his friend's shoulder as he was buttoning his waistcoat. "I heard from Merry and Sin that they met you at a gambling hell the other night. Is there a problem? I've got plenty of the ready, if you're in need."

St. John stopped dressing. "What?" He burst out laughing. "Oh no, Julian. No. Thank you. You *are* a good friend."

"But, Fungy... a gambling hell, and now a card party? If you're not in debt, then why this sudden interest?"

"It is... er, well, I'm afraid you will just have to wait to find out. I'm sorry, Julian, truly I am, but I can't tell you just now," St. John said.

He did wish that he could have been more honest. Perhaps he would have even been able to enlist Julian's aid in catching Kirtland. But St. John just could not do so—not without speaking to Lord Halsbury first.

And besides, he did so want to be the one who caught him. It had to be entirely St. John's work that brought Kirtland to justice. A wonderful chill of excitement and anticipation ran through him.

"You'll just have to trust me," he told Julian. "I'm not in debt or in any sort of trouble, I assure you. You'll learn it all before too long, if my suspicions are correct."

He wrote a quick note to Lord Halsbury, sending it off with his man before grabbing his coat and putting it on as he headed out the door. "Come along now, I can't afford to be late," he said, as if it had been Julian who was stalling them.

Julian laughed as he followed him out the door.

Twenty-Six

St. John walked into Lady Kemble's with Julian close on his heels. Perhaps, he thought, still glowing with excitement, his friend assumed that sticking close to him was the way to get at the bottom of all of his elusiveness.

However, all it did was to make him bump right into St. John when he stopped short just inside the door to the drawing room.

Nearly every eye was trained on two remarkably dressed ladies. The first was in a deep red domino, the second in a faded, rather shabby blue cloak. They were standing on the far side of the room having an argument, albeit a whispered one. The lady in blue even went so far as to try and grab the arm of the lady in red and pull her away.

A flash of gold on her wrist had St. John rushing to the scene. He knew that bracelet, and Fungy could never allow Miss Grace to embarrass herself in public.

"Good evening, ladies," he said smoothly but quietly, approaching them just before their hostess did. "I believe it would be best if you took your argument outside."

He then turned to Lady Kemble. "Do not worry, ma'am, I will ensure that there will be no further disruption to your party."

Lady Kemble looked very relieved. She clearly had not relished the thought of having to deal with the altercation herself. "Oh, thank you, Fungy. I always know that I can count on you."

St. John gave her a little bow, and firmly took each lady by her elbow and led them both out onto the terrace. Julian followed closely behind.

St. John's job had just gotten much more difficult. He hadn't expected to find Rose here this evening and hadn't even considered the social ramifications Kirtland's downfall would have on her.

Naturally, once it was known throughout the *ton* that Kirtland was a crook, everyone would look askance at Rose, wondering if she had been an accomplice or just another innocent duped by him. Either way, her reputation would end up in tatters.

As soon as they were out of sight of the rest of the party, Rose threw back her hood. "Thank you, St. John. I was *attempting* to get my sister out of there, but she would not listen."

Laia, too, threw back her hood and mask, revealing her distinctive bright red hair. "I can't believe that you would want me to leave, when I was finally winning back the money that *you* lost!"

"It doesn't matter what you were doing. You should not have been there in the first place!" Both ladies were much too upset to get any further in their argument. They both clearly needed a minute to calm down, so he provided a diversion.

"Miss Laia, may I present my good friend, the Earl of Huntley?"

The girls stopped glaring at each other long enough to observe the social niceties and greet Julian.

Julian bowed over Laia's hand, using his usual pleasant and open charm to defuse the tension, as St.

John knew he would. "How lovely to meet you, Miss Laia. May I ask how you managed to get into the party? I assume you were not invited."

Laia gave a guilty little smile. "It was quite easy, actually, my lord. The back gate to the garden was open, so I just slipped in."

"You stole into a stranger's garden?" Rose was aghast.

"What if you had gone through the wrong gate?" Julian asked calmly.

"I counted the number of houses from the front, and then the number of garden doors in the back. And I figured if I'd gotten the wrong one, I could just slip away again," Laia explained with a little shrug of her shoulders.

"That was extremely bold of you," St. John said, "but now you must make your exit and do so as unobtrusively as possible. Through the front door this time."

"But I don't want to leave!" Laia protested.

"It doesn't matter what you want right now, Laia; it is the right thing to do," her sister said gently.

"I'm afraid you must always do the right thing, no matter how boring that is, Miss Laia, just as we discussed in the park the other day," St. John said, hoping that his influence would help to convince the girl, who had the look of a stubborn child just now.

"But I was winning!" Laia argued.

Winning? From Kirtland? St. John wondered what his game was, and how deeply involved Rose was.

"That's wonderful, Laia, but you shouldn't have been here in the first place. A seventeen–year–old girl cannot be allowed to attend, a card party, and especially not to gamble at one," Rose said with finality.

"Afraid she's right, Miss Laia. It is not strictly proper even for Rose to come to such things," St. John said, still holding out hope that she could be convinced to leave quietly.

"She did so once before," Laia pouted.

"Yes, but she was both here in a domino and escorted by a gentleman. The rules could be bent a little."

"Well, I am here in a domino," Laia said crossing her arms defiantly.

"But you should not be here at all," St. John explained, beginning to lose his patience.

"I would be happy to escort you home, Miss Laia," Julian offered.

St. John was beyond grateful for his friend's presence.

"Thank you, my lord, that is very kind of you," Rose said, accepting his offer without hesitation.

"But what about my game? I was winning," Laia complained yet again, now beginning to sound more like the child she still was.

"Your game is over, Laia," Rose said.

"But I've only won forty pounds," Laia said, clearly trying another tack to get her sister's permission to return to her game. "You still owe another sixty you can't pay. I've got to go back and try to win that money, Rose."

"No, you don't!" Rose and St. John said simultaneously.

St. John could not allow either Laia or her sister to go back to gambling with Lord Kirtland. If they had only lost one hundred pounds, they'd been lucky so far. But he could not allow them to risk any more money—money they clearly didn't have. He remembered that

Rose had told him that her family was financially strapped, but this wasn't the way to remedy that. More and more, St. John was wishing that Rose had never become entangled with Kirtland. The only way for her to come out of Kirtland's unmasking unscathed was for her distance herself from him right away. St. John just wasn't sure how he was going to convince her to do so without jeopardizing his entire investigation, or their friendship.

"But..."

"No, Laia. I told you, gambling is not the way to pay that debt," Rose said.

"Please listen to your sister, Miss Laia. If you continue to gamble with Lord Kirtland, you will only get further and further into debt," St. John said, grateful that Rose had learned this lesson quickly. Now it was up to her sister to do so.

Laia looked from Rose to St. John, clearly at a loss. "But I was winning."

"I assure you, it wouldn't have continued," St. John said as gently as he could.

"You don't know that," Laia said.

"Yes, I do." St. John stopped. He could not tell them what he had learned about Lord Kirtland. But how could he not?

This assignment was becoming more onerous by the moment.

But first things first. Laia *had* to go home.

"Julian, I think now would be an excellent time for you to escort Miss Laia home."

Julian bowed to the young lady, who was still very reluctant to go.

"Please, Miss Laia," Julian said very gently but firmly, while holding out his arm for her to take.

With a pout, she put her hood and mask back on. Taking his arm, she allowed him to escort her back into the house.

Rose turned to St. John as soon as her sister was gone. "I don't know how to thank you, St. John…"

"You won't thank me once you hear what I need to tell you."

He must have been frowning, for Rose continued. "What is it? Do you think that Laia's reputation has already been destroyed by this? As long as no one finds out it was she…"

St. John wiped the expression off his face. "No. It is not that. This concerns Lord Kirtland." St. John took a deep breath. "Can you think of any reason why Lord Kirtland would want to win money from you, Rose?" He asked, delaying the inevitable. But indeed, He *couldn't* figure out why Kirtland had involved Rose in the first place. Why had he targeted her? She was not an heiress.

Rose paused, looking very confused. She shook her head slowly. "He has not won money from me; it was Mr. Aiken to whom I lost. Lord Kirtland was kind enough to write a vowel to him for me, which is how I came to owe the money to him instead."

St. John nodded. "Yes, but there still has to be a reason why he wanted you indebted to him."

And then it hit him. "Ah! It isn't *you* he wants under his thumb, it must be Lord Pemberton–Howe."

"What? What are you…"

St. John looked at Rose intently. "Kirtland is an archaeologist. He probably needs your father's name to lend credit to his own archaeological aspirations." And was it possible that Rose hadn't confided the state of her family's finances to Kirtland as she had done with him? That would explain it too if Kirtland thought she was wealthy.

"Well, of course, he will receive any help he needs from my father. We are to be married."

"But you should not," Fungy said bluntly.

"But... what do you mean? I thought you were happy for me!" Her cheeks began to turn pink. "It was you who made it possible."

"I know! I am, well, I *was* happy for you." St. John didn't know how much he dared reveal, but he had to protect her.

"And now?"

"Now I have learned something that makes it impossible for you to marry him." St. John took a deep breath and braced himself for any possible response—it was unlikely that she was going to take this with any sort of equanimity. "Rose, I am very sorry, but you need to end your engagement with Lord Kirtland."

"What? Why? St. John..."

He took hold of her hands. "Please, Rose, just listen to me. You know I wouldn't ask this of you if it wasn't extremely important. You *must* break off your engagement."

"Actually, I believe it is your relationship with her which must be broken, Fotheringay–Phipps."

St. John spun around, pulling Rose behind him, to face Roland Egerton.

"I don't know what nonsense you are putting into my fiancée's head, but I believe I've had enough of your interference in my life," Lord Kirtland said, strolling toward them in a way that was entirely too menacing for St. John's comfort.

"Not nonsense, Kirtland. Sound advice," St. John said standing his ground. He knew he was perfectly able to protect Rose, even though Kirtland had probably as much as thirty pounds on him. His fight with Merry had proven that he was a fully capable pugilist when necessary.

Rose pulled her hand out of his grasp and stepped from behind him. Of course, he couldn't protect her if she didn't want to be protected, he realized with a sinking heart.

She didn't say anything, just looked from him to Kirtland and back again. He wished he could tell her what he knew. He wished he could accuse Kirtland to his face, right here, right now, but Lord Halsbury's response to his note had reached him just as he and Julian had arrived at this little card party — specifically telling him to wait until Halsbury could arrive with the proper authorities.

Lord Kirtland reached forward and took Rose's hand. Tucking it into the crook of his arm as if he owned her. "Stay away," he commanded Fungy. He turned and walked back into the party with Rose at his side.

She didn't say anything. Not a word. And St. John hadn't been able to tell what she'd been thinking from her expression. Had she wanted to go with Kirtland? Had she even considered doing as St. John had said, despite his lack of a clear reason, and breaking it off with him?

No. Her silence had said it all. She was, implicitly, sweetly, and with all the gentleness that was inherent in her, breaking things off with St. John.

His heart sank to his feet. Perhaps it was better this way. She would be hating him soon enough when she learned what he was going to be accusing her fiancé of this evening.

Twenty-Seven

Rose sat, stitching quietly, in the corner of the drawing room. Every so often a tear would fall, unbidden, onto her work. She did not try to stop them.

After the events of last night, both of her sisters had left her alone. She was certain that Laia was still upset that she had been forced to leave the party, and it was likely she'd told Thalia everything, including how unfair Rose and St. John had been to her.

They sat with their backs to her by the empty hearth.

But they didn't know what had occurred after Laia had left.

How could St. John have been so cruel to her last night? Didn't he realize that Lord Kirtland was the only person who could save her family from financial ruin? And to ask her to break things off with him... for what reason? She just couldn't fathom.

He hadn't had a chance to tell her why before Lord Kirtland had joined them, but she'd been so hurt by what St. John was asking her to do that she hadn't been able to say anything. He knew she needed to marry for money. How could he put her in such a difficult position?

She wasn't doing this for herself. Her blinders about Lord Kirtland had come off the day they'd gone for a ride in the park with her sisters. But there was nothing she could do. She *had* to marry him. How could St. John do this to her?

Rose put down her embroidery to blow her nose.

She jumped as the drawing room door abruptly flew open, banging against the adjacent wall.

"My dear..." Aunt Farmington nearly ran into the room and then stopped short. She scanned the room and then found Rose sitting in the corner.

"Oh, my dear Rose, you simply would not believe what I have heard!" she exclaimed, walking briskly over. Rose had never seen the older woman move so quickly. Surely there was something seriously wrong.

Rose stood up. "What is it, Aunt? What has happened?"

Thalia and Laia had also jumped up at their aunt's dramatic entrance.

"Is it Papa? Has something happened to him?" Thalia cried.

Aunt Farmington turned on the girl. "Your Papa? No, why, have you heard something?"

"No, only you seem to be very upset about some news. I thought it might be..."

"Oh, no. It is Lord Kirtland," she said, turning back to Rose.

"Lord Kirtland? What about him?" Rose asked.

"He and Mr. Aiken have fled the country! Everyone is talking about it! Apparently the two of them have been working together to cheat at cards. They were caught last night at Lady Kemble's card party by..." she paused dramatically. "You will never guess!"

"Fungy?" Rose whispered.

Aunt Farmington deflated. "Yes! How did you know?"

A Dandy In Disguise

"He mentioned something to me the last time I saw him," she said. She knew her voice sounded hollow, but she simply could not gather up the emotional energy to put any life into it.

Rose dropped back down into her chair. That's what he had wanted to warn her about. Why he had told her to distance herself from Lord Kirtland. He knew what was about to happen. He had wanted to protect her.

Her tear started flowing in earnest. He was trying to save her—yet again!

"Oh, my dear, I am so glad that you were not present. It would have been beyond humiliating. Apparently, Mr. Fotheringay-Phipps was very clever about it," her aunt said, warming to her story once again. "He asked Lord Kirtland to write down the name of his tailor, then when the authorities came, he showed that that handwriting and the handwriting of some note he'd written earlier incriminating himself matched!"

Thalia and Laia both gasped and Rose noticed that they were both sitting at the very edge of their seats, obviously completely enjoying the story.

"It was then that chaos broke out. Kirtland shoved Mr. Fotheringay-Phipps, while his accomplice, Mr. Aiken, shoved Lord Halsbury aside and they both escaped!" she finished dramatically.

"Oh, what a shame!" Thalia exclaimed.

"Thalia, that is not at all charitable," Rose admonished, although she secretly had to agree considering how nasty Lord Kirtland had been to her and her sisters.

"No, but I'm in complete agreement with her," Laia said, nodding to their youngest sister.

"Well, it is just a shame that the whole ordeal happened at all, is what I say. Nearly everyone knows that you were engaged to Lord Kirtland," she finished turning back to Rose.

"They do?" Rose asked, dismayed.

Her aunt had the grace to look slightly discomforted. "Oh well, of course. We were all so happy that you'd made such a good match. Why, I must have told at least ten people — and then, of course, they would have gone about telling people, and well, you know how it is."

Lady Farmington tsked sadly and shook her head. "Who would have known that such a pleasant gentleman would do such a thing? And we all thought he was wealthy! Why, he must have been as poor as a church mouse!"

"Not if he was cheating at cards," Thalia said frankly. "That would have made him quite wealthy, I imagine."

"What are you going to do, Rose?" Laia asked.

Rose felt as if her head was in a thick fog. She shook her head and sniffed back her tears, but she just could not focus her mind on the overwhelming news and its consequences. She over at her sister. "I don't know. I'm not sure there is anything I can do."

"Well, no, of course not. The gentleman in question having fled the country, your engagement is, naturally, at an end." Aunt Farmington said, handing Rose her handkerchief and then moving to sit down on the sofa now that her news was told.

"Thalia, dear, ring for some tea," her aunt requested, now sounding very tired.

"That means that we no longer have a way to pay our bills," Thalia pointed out needlessly as she walked to the door to pull the bell cord.

"And there aren't any other wealthy gentlemen for Rose to marry," Laia added.

"Not only that, my dears, but no man would even consider becoming engaged to your sister now. Well, at least not for a good long time. The stigma, you know," Aunt Farmington added, wiping delicately at the corners of her eyes with another handkerchief she'd pulled from her reticule. "And I am afraid it may rub off on Thalia and Laia as well. None of you will have an easy time of it, I fear."

With that bit of news, Rose completely lost hold of the tenuous control over her emotions. A shot of pure anguish racked her body, and her sisters rushed to her side as a wracking sob burst from her.

"I have failed," she whispered through her tears, "I have failed you all!"

"Oh, no, Rose." Laia caressed her hair. "Not at all."

"You still have Fungy," Thalia offered.

Rose began to cry again, "No, I don't. He told me to end my engagement, but Lord Kirtland overheard him and pulled me away. And I...I didn't say anything. I just went with him."

"But why did you do something so stupid?" Thalia asked, bewildered.

Rose just shook her head and scrubbed at her tears. "Lord Kirtland is all that we have... all that we *had* standing between us and the poor house, or, or debtor's prison. I don't...didn't want to marry him, I *had* to marry him. How could St. John not have known that? Why didn't he tell me what Lord Kirtland had done earlier? I would have broken my engagement with him if I had known." Rose hit her leg with her fist, her tears turning to anger.

"I thought Fungy loved you," Laia said, wiping her own tears from her cheeks.

"He is horrible," Thalia agreed vehemently. "Some friend he turned out to be! Why I could…"

"No, Thalia," Laia interrupted her.

"You can't do anything, Thalia. I don't even know what *I* can do," Rose said, trying to hold back a fresh wave of tears and failing miserably.

Twenty-Eight

St. John sipped at his brandy. He hadn't taken the time to enjoy the quiet, unobtrusive company at Whites in a while. But then, he had been rather preoccupied the past few weeks.

He nearly laughed to himself at the understatement, and if things had worked out differently perhaps he would have actually laughed. But not now.

He could not fathom how he was going to live without seeing Rose. He knew, of course, that she would never want to see him again after he was responsible for ruining her life. He had known when he'd asked her to break her engagement that he would be risking his friendship with her. He'd had to try to save her, and perhaps he would have succeeded if Kirtland hadn't chosen that exact moment to step in.

Despite everything, though, he still loved her. She had become a vital part of his life, so much so that just the thought of never seeing her again—

St. John finished off the rest of the brandy in one gulp.

His only hope at this point was that her silence hadn't been as condemning he'd thought. Perhaps she just *couldn't* have said anything? Perhaps if he'd had a chance to explain...

St. John nearly jumped as a voice intruded into his thoughts. "Fungy, what are you doing sitting here all alone?" Sin settled into the chair beside him, as St. John sank back into his..

Mustering up a smile, he glanced over at Sin. "Just enjoying a moment's peace."

"Been busy since that whole Kirtland business, I suppose?"

"Yes. I can't tell you how many times I've been asked to repeat the story of how I figured out that it was he who was leading the gambling scheme."

Merry and Julian walked over and joined them with a footman and a bottle of brandy in tow.

"Must be hard being a hero," Merry laughed, sitting down and pouring out the brandy for all of them.

St. John paused and looked for a moment at Sin, Merry, and Julian.

This was the way it was supposed to be, he thought to himself. This was right. He was in pain, and in need of companionship and perhaps some good, sound advice. He was in need of his friends—and here they were, without fail.

What a relief it was, after all his doubts! His heart felt immeasurably lighter than it had been not five minutes ago.

St. John smiled for just an instant and shook his head. "I'm not a hero. I was doing a job I was asked to do."

"Speaking of which, I've got a bone to pick with you, Cousin!" Merry said, putting down the bottle before he had finished filling all of the glasses.

St. John held up his hands preemptively. "I plead innocence."

"How could you have accepted a position to work with Parliament without telling any of us?"

"Well, it wasn't really with Parliament, just with Halsbury."

"Yes, and he was working on Parliament's behalf."

St. John shrugged. "It was a secret investigation. I couldn't tell you."

As Merry picked up the brandy bottle once more, Sin commented, "I just can't believe you've let us go on believing you to be nothing more than a society buck—and all this time you've been ferreting out master criminals."

St. John felt his old resentments flash to the surface. But he knew that Sin meant well, and so forced himself to speak lightly. "Well, if you'd remember, I haven't always been so consumed by fashion. There was a time when I was more concerned with my studies than even you were about yours."

Sin and Merry began laughing. "I remember those days!"

"My God, what a bore you were at times, harping on about reading this playwright or that philosopher! At least you *did* take time out to have some fun with us every so often." Merry shook his head.

"We were practically inseparable!" St. John exclaimed.

"Yes, but you were always harping on about your studies," Sin complained.

"I loved the classics." "Still do, I suppose," Julian said.

"Do you?" Merry asked.

"I've caught him twice over the past few weeks," Julian said, helping himself to a glass. "Once reading Greek, and quoting it to me! And the other day, writing in it."

"I can't believe you've kept that up," Sin commented, shaking his head.

"I think there's a lot about me that you've forgotten, or just don't realize," St. John said quietly, looking at Merry.

Merry had the grace to look uncomfortable for a moment. "Fungy, after what Miss Grace said, I've been thinking…"

He held up his hand. "It's all right, Merry. I've already beaten you to a bloody pulp about it. Although I must admit, you choosing Sin to be the baby's godfather certainly got me thinking. It hurt, but it made me take a good hard look at my life." He paused to take a sip of his brandy. "Well, that and nearly drowning."

"Drowning? When did that happen?" Merry asked, sitting forward.

St. John told them briefly about saving Miss Thalia Grace from the river and the consequences—how it had been the final straw in his decision to make some major changes in his life.

His friends were all stunned into silence, until Merry finally said, "I can't believe you didn't tell us."

St. John looked down at the brandy in his glass. "You were all so busy with your own lives. We haven't been seeing very much of each other recently."

"It's true," Sin said slowly.

"I can't change the demands my family are making on me…" Merry began.

"Nor should you. Teresa needs you, and you should be there for her, no matter what."

"But that doesn't mean that you can't come over and share your problems with me, St. John," his cousin said, earnestly. "I'm still here."

St. John nodded. "Thank you."

Sin and Julian immediately both concurred.

"Well, then, perhaps you all can think of a way out of a little dilemma I seem to be facing right now," St. John said, giving his friends a smile.

"Anything!"

"You met Miss Grace at my little picnic last week," St. John began.

"Became engaged to Kirtland that day, didn't she?" Sin asked.

St. John nodded. "That was the whole point of the party. I'd gone to her home to ask her to marry me, and... well, before I could utter a word, she told me she was hoping for a proposal from Kirtland."

"You were going to propose to her?" Merry was astonished.

"Finally found someone to make you forget Georgiana," Sin said approvingly.

St. John gave him a little smile. "With Georgiana's full approval, naturally."

"But now that Kirtland is gone, Miss Grace is free again," Julian pointed out.

"Exactly," St. John said. "Only problem is, I tried to warn her about Kirtland before Halsbury showed up, but Kirtland interrupted us and I didn't get a chance. He told me to stay away from Rose and then walked away with her. Or—she walked away with him. I'm not sure."

"Oh, dear," Julian said.

"Makes things a little difficult," Merry agreed.

"Not going to give up, are you?" Sin asked.

St. John smiled. "No!"

His friends laughed approvingly at that, and then huddled together.

"We'll come up with something. Have no fear, Fungy," Julian said, giving him a pat on the shoulder.

"That's just what I was counting on."

Twenty-Nine

Rose was just finishing her sampler when her aunt joined her in the drawing room the following day.

"Have you given a thought to what you will wear this evening?" Aunt Farmington asked.

Rose looked up. "I was not planning on going out this evening." Not after the countless hours of sleep she had lost the past few nights just thinking about St. John.

She could still see his sad face in her mind's eye when she had walked away with Lord Kirtland. It haunted her—her happy, always smiling St. John looking so miserable. If she had only said something, anything...

"What do you mean? Tonight is Lady Wynworth's rout. You *must* attend," her aunt said, erasing the horrible picture from Rose's mind and bringing her back to the present.

"If I go, I'm certain to be the laughingstock of the party," Rose said, stabbing her needle through the cloth savagely.

And if she went, she would surely meet St. John.

What would she do if she were to meet him? Would she have to turn away? Would he? No, there was no way around it. The best thing to do would be to simply not go to any more society parties.

The thought of life without St. John...

Rose squeezed her eyes shut for a moment to stop the stinging of her tears.

"And if you do not go, do you think it will be any better?" her aunt asked.

Rose kept her eyes down. "No, but at least I won't have to hear the horrible things that people are saying about me."

"Rose Grace, do not tell me that you are afraid to face your detractors!"

Rose blinked her eyes clear, set down her sewing once again, looked straight at her aunt and said, "I am afraid to face my detractors."

And St. John.

Aunt Farmington laughed. "No, you are not. And if you are, I shall not allow you to be. You *will* attend the rout this evening."

"No..." Rose began, but was interrupted by the butler, who walked into the room, followed by Lady Huntley and Lady Reath — the wives of St. John's friends. Could it have only been a week ago that she'd met them?

"I beg your pardon, ma'am, but Miss Grace has visitors." He announced the ladies and then left the room. Rose stood up to greet them.

"What a pleasant surprise! Please come in," Aunt Farmington said to the two ladies.

"Thank you," Lady Huntley said, her bright blue eyes looking openly and sympathetically at Rose.

"We came by to see how you were, Miss Grace," Lady Reath explained, settling her petite frame on the sofa, "and to ask if you were planning on attending Lady Wynworth's party this evening." She was as direct and straightforward as Rose remembered.

Aunt Farmington gave Rose a significant look.

A Dandy In Disguise

"I was not planning on doing so," Rose said, ignoring her aunt.

"But you must!" Lady Reath said, emphatically.

"Yes, really," Lady Huntley added, in a quieter tone. "If you do not, your position in society will be thoroughly jeopardized."

"And everyone may think that you knew about Lord Kirtland's dishonest activities," Lady Reath added bluntly.

Rose was taken aback by this. "Do you really think so?" she asked, beginning to be seriously worried. It was not only her reputation at stake, after all, but that of her sisters and father as well.

"Absolutely," they said together.

"I told you, my dear, you *must* attend this rout," Aunt Farmington said, adding her voice to their argument.

Rose looked from one lady to the next. But if she went... how was she to avoid St. John? Did she *really* want to avoid him? If she went, she might see him again.

Lady Huntley gave her a warm smile. "Do not worry, Miss Grace. We will be there with you, and between us and our husbands, no one will dare to say anything unkind to you."

Rose returned her smile gratefully. "Thank you, my lady. You are much too kind."

The thought of not seeing St. John ever again was unbearable. And just thinking about being with him made her heart feel so much lighter and happier. She would decide later what she would say to him—if she was given the opportunity... if he didn't turn his back on her the way she had to him that awful, awful night when he'd tried to warn her.

"Not really. We just care about..."

"It is no problem at all," Lady Huntley said, interrupting Lady Reath and giving her a fierce look. "Now, first of all, you must agree to call us by our given names, and we shall call you by yours, for we are going to be fast friends before you know it."

Rose nodded her head and laughed, feeling better already. Somehow, with the support of these two very kind ladies, she felt as if she could face nearly anything—social opprobrium and St. John.

"And secondly," Lady Huntley — Cassandra — continued, "you must show us what you are going to wear, because, as I am certain you know, you must look magnificent to face down the *ton.*"

And bowl St. John over as well, Rose couldn't help but add to herself.

Rose could not deny that she was nervous that evening when she entered Lady Wynworth's party. She still hadn't decided what to say to St. John when they met. She thought that maybe she would try to apologize, but that seemed to be too little. Of course, throwing herself at his feet would be a bit overdramatic.

She smiled at the thought, but with an edge of panic in her mind. She needed some sort of happy medium, but so far she hadn't hit on just the right thing.

But there was one thing that Rose could deny no longer—St. John Fotheringay–Phipps had become such an integral part of her life that she could not imagine it without him. And tonight, she had to do everything and anything she could to get him back into it—even if it did mean literally throwing herself at his feet.

Rose and her aunt met Cassandra and her husband, Lord Huntley, just inside the door to Lady Wynworth's main drawing room, as they'd arranged.

"Excellent, Rose. I knew that green gown would look stunning on you! And the new gold trim really makes you stand out," Cassandra said, looking Rose over approvingly.

Rose swallowed nervously. "Thank you. I promise to buy you more of this wonderful trimming as soon as..."

"Pish–posh! Don't even think about it. I told you this afternoon, I bought it on a whim and didn't even know which dress I might sew it on to. It looks perfect on you—and I'm happy that I had something to liven up your dress. Cutting the neckline down has helped a great deal as well, just as I told you it would."

Rose could feel her face heat when she thought about how much décolletage she was displaying this evening. However, as had been pointed out by Cassandra and Sara, it was no more than every other lady present, and a good deal less than some.

Cassandra turned to her husband, who was looking quite handsome—his black coat setting off his black hair, dark complexion and stunning bright blue–green eyes. Of course, Rose much preferred St. John's dark blond locks and laughing blue eyes, but Lord Huntley's looks were striking, especially when next to his fair wife.

"Rose is looking quite pretty, isn't she, Julian?" Cassandra said.

Lord Huntley bowed. "I could not agree more, my love. Very pretty, Miss Grace, you are looking very pretty."

Rose felt her face grow warm, but she curtsied and mumbled her thanks.

Lord Reath and his wife, Sara, joined them just then, so Rose had to endure another round of compliments and exclamations over how good the new trimming looked on her dress. If Rose didn't know they honestly meant well, she would have thought that they were overdoing it just a little. But after having spent the afternoon with both ladies, she knew they had only the best intentions for her.

"You clearly have no need of me this evening, Rose. I shall leave you to your friends," her aunt said, before setting off to find one of her own numerous friends.

Rose watched her go with a little trepidation. Without her aunt there to support her, she would be completely dependent on her new friends to see her through what was sure to be a difficult evening. She sincerely hoped her trust was not misplaced.

Thirty

The group of friends proceeded further into the overcrowded room and approached the dance floor where a country dance was just forming.

"Would one of the most beautiful ladies in attendance grant me the honor of this dance?" a gentleman said, coming up just next to Rose.

She turned to see Lord Merrick bowing to her, a twinkle of mischief in his eyes.

Rose laughed and flushed once again. "La, sir, you could not be referring to me," she said, jumping right into playing his game.

"But who else would I be speaking to?" he asked.

Rose looked to her other side, where Cassandra was standing and watching this lighthearted play. "Why, to Lady Huntley, of course," Rose said, stepping aside so that Cassandra was closer to Lord Merrick.

He shook his head. "She is indeed one of the prettier ladies present, but I believe Julian might be tempted to call me out if I were to tell her so."

Rose and Cassandra laughed. Lord Huntley, upon hearing his name, turned back to them to see what was going on, but Lord Merrick could not be put off so easily. Once again, he held out his hand to Rose.

"Oh yes, do dance with Merry, Rose," Cassandra said at once. "It will do wonders for your reputation. You must be seen dancing with as many gentlemen as possible. That way, the gossips will not have so much fodder to chew on." Rose could see her point—the more she was seen as being accepted, especially by gentlemen in as good a social position as Lord Merrick, the better it would be.

Gratefully, she took Lord Merrick's hand and allowed him to lead her onto the dance floor. Cassandra and Lord Huntley followed them.

Rose felt as if the entire room was watching as she and Lord Merrick turned and skipped about in the dance. If it were not for his reassuring smiles and for Cassandra next to her, she was sure she would have succumbed to the temptation to run and hide in the ladies withdrawing room.

It had not been above two minutes after the dance ended that Lady Jersey approached Rose with a little smirk on her face.

"Good evening, Miss Grace. I must say, I am surprised to see you here," she said.

"Surely you would not expect her to shut herself away because she had been deceived along with everybody else?" St. John said, strolling up to them at a leisurely pace.

Rose spun around. *St. John!*

Lady Jersey turned to face her opponent a polite smile hovering on her lips. . "You always believe the best in everyone, Fungy."

He gave a little bow. "Indeed, I do. Believe that you would not wish to destroy a girl's reputation simply because she misjudged a fellow, as you did yourself, Lady Jersey. You were the one who insisted on granting him vouchers to Almack's, were you not?"

The lady blushed a dull red. "Well, anyone can make a mistake. Why, we were all taken in by Lord Kirtland."

"Yes, indeed, we were." St. John turned to Rose as Lady Jersey moved on quickly.

Rose started to breathe again, not even having fully realized that she'd stopped

St. John took her hand gently in his and looked at her with genuine concern. "How *are* you, Rose?"

"Much better now that you are here," she said, quietly, and then realized that she had spoken her thoughts out loud. She stole her hand back from St. John and pressed it to her now flaming cheeks.

St. John just laughed. "Can't tell you how happy I am to hear that."

"St. John..." Rose began. But he gave his head a quick shake as if to say, 'not here'.

The orchestra played the introduction to a waltz. St. John held out his hand and gave her a small bow. "Would you care to dance, Miss Grace?"

"Er, oh, yes. Thank you." Rose answered with a curtsey.

Once again, as they made their way to the dance floor, Rose felt as if every eye was on her. She was sure of it when she looked about her and saw Lady Jersey and Countess Lieven standing by the side, watching her, whispering to each other.

"Do not pay them any mind," St. John said firmly.

She looked back at him. He was smiling and looking like he hadn't a care in the world—just like always.

"Perhaps if you stopped looking like a frightened deer, and instead placed a smile on your beautiful lips, it might help."

Rose gave a little laugh. "I'm sorry."

"No need to apologize. That's better." He nodded approvingly as Rose relaxed a little and tried to look as if she were enjoying herself.

It wasn't easy. She felt as if every muscle in her body was wound tight with tension. What was she going to say to him? She had never worked it out, and now...

"Is that a new dress? It is extremely flattering," St. John said, as he gently turned her around with the movement of the dance.

Rose wanted to hug him. He was so wonderful, talking of nothing at all just to ease her tensions.

"No, actually, it is an old dress, but altered a little and with new trimming added. Sara... Lady Reath and Lady Huntley came and helped me with it this afternoon."

St. John nodded, a smile tugging up one corner of his mouth. "Well, it is extremely becoming. Your sister Laia should try wearing such a creation. It would enhance her coloring in a very flattering way."

"I shall have to see about that."

They continued to turn about the room, sharing an easy silence. The voices all around them seemed to fade away. Even Lady Jersey's shrill voice, which was so easy to hear even from a distance, faded to nothing.

It no longer mattered to Rose what other people were saying about her. The only person she cared about was St. John.

She had to say something to him, and she had to say it now. "St. John..." Rose began again, not even entirely sure of what she was going to say.

He shook his head. "Do not even think about it, Rose. You could not have known."

How did he know what she was thinking?

"But I didn't even..."

"Entirely understandable," he said.

Rose looked up at him and wondered how anyone could be so wonderful.

"You had no idea what I was doing, or why," he continued quietly. "How could you know?"

"I should have said something."

"Kirtland was your fiancé. What could you have said?" He paused. His voice got quieter, so that Rose had to lean forward a bit to hear him. "He had your affection. It was he who you wanted to marry. Not me. And it was because of that that it took me longer than it should have to figure out that it was, in fact, Kirtland who was the mastermind behind the gambling scheme."

He paused to allow her to go through the open French doors before him. He had waltzed her over to the other side of the room, and now led her outside to the garden.

Rose felt as if her head were spinning, but she walked out into the fragrant garden. It was filled with beautiful colored lanterns lining the walkways. St. John's hand was still on the small of her back as he guided her to one of the more remote corners of the garden.

"Georgiana was the one who told me that she thought Kirtland was more than he seemed. It was her suspicions that made me realize that it wasn't just my jealousy speaking—but that there was, in fact, a reason to be suspicious of him."

"Lady Mirthwood knew it was him?"

"No. She didn't know anything about my investigation. She just knew that there was something about Kirtland that made her feel uncomfortable. She is an excellent judge of character, you know."

"But he made me feel uncomfortable too. I thought..." Rose could not finish her sentence. She had thought that that feeling meant that she was in love. But now she was beginning to realize that love did not have to be uncomfortable.

In fact, she thought it could be very comfortable indeed.

"You think a great deal," he said quietly.

St. John was standing very close to her now. His warmth beside her made Rose not only feel comfortable, but safe and secure. She wanted nothing more than rest her head on his shoulder and feel him wrap his arms securely around her.

"Too much," she agreed.

He bent down and very gently pressed his lips to hers.

Immediately, Rose felt a rush of tingles through her body. Warmth followed, welling up in her breast. Without worrying about what he would think of her, or whether or not she was doing the right thing, she allowed herself to just relax and kiss him back. She found that she needed to wrap her arms around his neck and hold onto him—just so that her knees wouldn't completely give way.

It felt so good, so right to be in St. John's arms.

Perhaps this, too, was love? This warm, wonderful feeling of being with a man who didn't put her on edge, but instead took the edge away and made her feel treasured and comforted.

"Rose," St. John said, when they finally separated. "I know you were in love with Lord Kirtland, but perhaps..."

"But I don't know that I was," Rose interrupted.

"You don't?"

A Dandy In Disguise

"No. I told you, I needed to marry Lord Kirtland because he was wealthy. It was the only way for our family to be able to pay our bills. I know how he made me feel, but it was nothing like this, St. John. You make me feel... cherished... loved."

St. John ran his fingers lightly down her cheek. "You do so much for your family. Don't you think it's time you did something for yourself instead?"

Rose looked down, focusing on the buttons of St. John's coat. "My family means everything to me. And it's expected..."

"Stop right there." He placed a finger on her lips. You are a sweet and generous person, but sometimes, my love, you need to think of yourself first and not worry about others." He lifted her chin so that her eyes met his. "Like now. Say that you will marry me."

Rose had to laugh and shake her head. This was one of the things she loved about St. John, he always saw the best in people. "I suppose my family can learn to manage with perhaps only a little help."

"I'll do what I can. But my heart is entirely yours."

St. John's lips pressed against hers once again, sending even more tingles down her body. She pressed herself even closer to him as he in turn drew her against him.

A discreet cough and a giggle made them jump apart.

"Er, thought you might be needing a chaperon," Lord Merrick said.

"Or six," Lady Merrick added, still giggling.

Rose felt her color rise as she realized that all of St. John's friends and their wives were standing about, discreetly admiring the flowers and the colored lanterns.

"And I seem to remember a certain cousin of mine reprimanding me for hanging on my wife's arm a few years ago," Lord Merrick said, with laughter in his voice.

St. John too began to laugh. "Back when I didn't know any better, I assure you, Cousin."

"Well, at least they don't always argue with each other," Lord Reath said, giving his wife a significant look.

"Well, but he doesn't try to manage her life for her at every turn," she said laughing, as she reached out to take her husband's hand affectionately.

"And they are both impeccably dressed," Cassandra said.

"And can quote Greek to each other to their heart's content," Lord Huntley added.

"Yes, I think they make a perfect match," Lord Merrick said.

"Shall we place a wager on it—perhaps over a hand of whist?" St. John asked.

"NO!" came the reply, loudly and in unison.

Rose laughed, looking adoringly at her handsome, witty, clever St. John, and took his hand firmly in hers. Hand in hand, they joined the three other couples, the sound of merry laughter warmly cocooning them all.

St. John gave her one last adoring look before he turned to leave. He'd been so sweet to bring her and Aunt Farmington home and then walk them to the door. Both her aunt and the footman had been discreet enough to leave them alone to say goodnight to each other.

Just as St. John reached for the door, however, it burst open. St. John jumped back, just barely missing getting hit by the swinging door.

"Oh! Fungy!" Rose's father bounded into the house. "Rose, good! Are your sisters still up as well? I got here as quickly as I could."

"Sir?" St. John asked.

"Papa, what's happened?" Rose said, coming forward.

"Call your sisters... no, I will," her father said. He then stood at the bottom of the stairs and bellowed, "Graces! Come down, I've got news!"

"Er, sir? If I could have a word with you as well," St. John said.

"Eh? Yes?" Lord Pemberton–Howe turned on him, but before St. John could say anything more, Laia and Thalia both came running down the stairs pulling on their wrappers.

"Papa!" Thalia said, ready to throw herself into her father's arms.

"What is it? What's happened?" Laia said.

"Oh!" they said in unison the minute the saw St. John standing there as well.

"Imagine you want to ask for my permission to marry my daughter?" Lord Pemberton–Howe said, smiling from St. John to Rose and then back again.

"Er, yes! But, how....?" St. John asked.

Her father just patted Rose on her cheek and said, "Knew you wouldn't be so stupid as to marry that Kirtland fellow. I must say, I never liked him."

He then went into his library, followed by St. John, the three girls and their Aunt Farmington who'd also come running at his bellow.

"I can't say that I did either after the way he treated my sisters," Rose admitted, "but we all thought he was wealthy enough to get us out of our troubles."

"Yes, well, that's not important any more, now is it? You can marry whoever you want, er, as long as it's Fungy. I do like him," her father said, laughing a little and giving St. John a hearty pat on his back.

St. John gave him a big smile and reached for Rose's hand.

"Why is it not important any longer, Papa?" Thalia asked.

"Ah! Yes!" He settled himself into a chair by the empty fireplace. "I have been to Pemberton, just as I told you... er, I did tell you that that's where I was going, didn't I?"

"You mentioned it briefly before leaving," Rose said.

"Yes? Well, that's where I was. Turns out that steward of mine, Mr. Strate, was not so straight after all. He's been fudging the books for the past ten years, and making a tidy profit on it too."

"Oh, no!" the three girls gasped.

"Oh, my lord, what did you do?" Aunt Farmington said, sitting down in the chair opposite his.

"I had to go down, naturally, and catch him at it. Squire Thompson and I managed to find most of the money Strate had squirreled away."

"But that's wonderful!" Rose cried, moving forward, but still holding on to St. John's hand since she just couldn't bear to let him go.

"No, Rosebud, it is not just wonderful, it's fantastic!" her father said excitedly, leaning forward. "It means that we now have enough money to pay all of our bills and more! And it means you can marry your young man here without a care."

Lord Pemberton–Howe sat back again, smiling at his dumbfounded family.

"It is fantastic," Rose agreed, blinking rapidly. She turned, and in front of her entire family, leaned forward and gave St. John a kiss on his smiling lips.

Also Available from Meredith Bond:
An Exotic Heir

Weaving a web of revenge can be satisfying, but dangerous to your heart.

London society is shallow and cruel, sending Cassandra Renwick running to Calcutta, the exotic seat of the British Raj. It's a fascinating place filled with interesting sights — including the dark and mysterious Julian Ritchie. But she never thought that an even greater heartbreak could be here in this alien and enchanting land.

Julian has always been discriminated against for being only half English. Embittered, he plots an intricate plan for vengeance with the innocent and lovely Cassandra as his pawn. But he soon finds that payback can be painful for the avenger as well when the threads of revenge unwittingly turn into the silken bonds of love.

And if you like a little magic in

your Regency romances

Magic In The Storm

Morgan is trapped and powerless.

The seventh child of the seventh child has always been a girl. Until Morgan Vallentyn was born. Because he's male he can't access the magical powers that should have been his. In order to attain his destiny, he first has to escape his home and find the source of his power — in the most unexpected of places.

Adriana would give up everything for her freedom.

Born to paint the natural world with unprecedented passion and vision, Adriana Hayden is bound by the laws of Regency society to her scheming guardian. But after meeting the handsome and mysterious Morgan, her world begins to open to enchanted possibilities she never could have imagined.

The only way to fulfill their destinies is for each to unlock the powers of the other — through the magic in the storm.

Continue on for an excerpt from **Magic In The Storm**

May, 1815

Adriana Hayden didn't even have to turn around. The quiet click of the door closing and the sigh of the sofa were all that she needed to hear to know that her dearest friend and companion, Henrietta, had come into the room.

She finished dabbing the black paint onto her canvas before stepping back and deciding that she had probably put too much. Well, she didn't care. It was perfect and it reflected her mood so precisely Adriana imagined she wouldn't even need to say a word to Henrietta.

She would paint the whole thing black if it wouldn't ruin what was turning out to be a rather nice depiction of a stormy sea. The water thundered, crashing with violence onto the rocks at the base of a sheer cliff. Menacing clouds hung overhead within moments of letting loose a torrent of rain.

"Oh dear," her companion said quietly, over the roar of the sea in Adriana's mind.

Adriana closed her eyes for a moment to stop them from stinging and then swallowed down the anger that had risen to the top of her throat again. "They wouldn't even let me see him," she said, without preamble.

"Who wouldn't?" Henrietta asked.

Adriana turned around into the quiet of the room. Henrietta was sitting, as always, with her back perfectly straight and her legs crossed at the ankle and tucked ever so slightly under the worn, comfortable sofa. Her brown hair was pulled up so tightly Adriana wondered that it didn't hurt, but her hazel eyes spoke volumes of sympathy, for which Adriana was grateful. Adriana resisted the urge to run up to her dear friend and throw her arms around her.

Instead, she lifted her chin and replied, "The clerk at Sir William's establishment."

"So you didn't even get to see Sir William? You didn't show him your work?"

Adriana shook her head and turned back to her painting. Carelessly, she dabbed more black paint on where it wasn't needed, darkening the sky even further.

"But that's not right!" Henrietta said, full of indignation for Adriana. "What reason did he give?"

Adriana couldn't even bear to turn around to face Henrietta again; the hurt was still too painful. She bit her lip to keep herself from either screaming in rage or crying like a thwarted child. She swallowed hard, again. "The clerk told me that he was certain that my watercolors were very pretty, but Sir William Agnew did not deal in a young lady's dabbling. He only sold the work of true artists." She paused at Henrietta's gasp, but then continued. "He suggested that I give my work to some handsome young gentleman in the hope that he will marry me."

"No, he didn't!"

"Oh, yes."

"Why, the nerve! The gall! The temerity of such... such..."

"A man," Adriana finished for her.

"An imbecile is what I was going to say."

"Perhaps they are one and the same," Adriana said, allowing her mouth to quirk up in a little smile.

Henrietta just harrumphed.

Adriana turned around and attempted to put a real smile onto her face. How was it that Henrietta always made her feel better? No matter what had upset her, Henrietta always slipped herself right up under Adriana's hurt and pried it away.

"It's all right, Henrietta. I'll just try someone else. I don't have to sell my paintings through Sir William. I'm certain there are plenty of other art dealers who will take a look at my work."

"But Sir William is the best," her friend argued.

"Yes, but another dealer will be able to sell my work just as well. He may not get the prices Sir William could command, but at least we'll get the money we need."

"Oh, Adriana, it's such a shame to have to sell your beautiful work..."

"But necessary. Absolutely necessary," she said with all of the conviction and certainty she felt, and that was substantial.

"You wouldn't have to sell so many or worry so much about price if you just left me..."

"I will not! How could you even suggest that I leave you here to deal with Lord Devaux yourself?" She took the few steps that separated them and knelt down on the floor at Henrietta's feet. "We will wait until I have enough money for both of us to survive. I will never leave you."

Henrietta squeezed Adriana's shoulder gratefully. "But..."

There was a knock at the door. Before Adriana could respond, Lord Devaux himself walked into the room.

About the Author

Meredith Bond is an award-winning author of a series of traditionally published Regency romances and indie-published paranormal romances. Known for her characters "who slip readily into one's heart," Meredith's heart belongs to her husband and two children. Along with writing romance, Meredith also teaches writing. If you would like a taste of her class in book form, **Chapter One** is available at your favorite e-retailer.

Want to know more? Come visit Meredith at her website, www.meredithbond.com or chat with her on Facebook (www.facebook.com/meredithbond fan) or Twitter (@merrybond).

If you'd like to be one of the first to know of Meredith's new releases, join her no-spamming email list at http://meredithbond.com/blog/ mailing-list.

Made in the USA
San Bernardino, CA
30 September 2014